Waking Virginia

By
Dorothea Hunt

D.H. PUBLISHING
ASHEVILLE

THE TANTRA SERIES BOOK ONE

Hunt, Dorothea.
Waking Virginia /
Dorothea Hunt.

ISBN: 978-0-9987230-4-4

Here and there is born a Saint Theresa,
foundress of nothing, whose loving heartbeats and sobs after an unattained
goodness tremble off and are dispersed
among hindrances, instead of centering in
some long-recognizable deed.

—George Eliot

Chapter One

Why are we so blind to our own motivations? I am starting to look a little pale around the eyes and at the edges of my lips. After all, I have just hung up with Professor Grange, the lonely genius perched high in the stacks of some library. He was short with me again today over the phone, but I suppose it may be this way with every great mind caught in the cruel frustration of staring into the depths of a blank page. He is waiting for the great insight to dawn. I am waiting for him to call me back to tell me what time I should pick him up from the airport.

Standing in front of my house, I loudly jangle the keys in the lock. I am trying to make as much noise as possible while entering the front door. I want to send my sister Jacqui the message that if she is slowly undressing one of her men on the couch, or perhaps caught in the clutches of total abandon, splayed out across the dining room table in the midst of some steamy sex scene, that she should move it into the bedroom, hurriedly, and to please tone it down a notch, or ten. Jacqui, as she likes to phrase it, "enjoys a healthy sex life," and I am in no mood to once again walk into the sounds of her deep, and satisfied moaning and groaning.

Mercifully, as I walk in, I spy Jacqui's bedroom door ajar and see her sitting pretty on her bed flipping through her latest *People* magazine, studiously digesting what's in and what's not, as if it actually matters. And for her it does, a great deal. What other people view as attractive and sexy is often on the forefront of my sister's mind; although for the life of me, I can't really imagine why. These are fads and fairly shallow ones at that. I believe there are more important things to focus on than which celebrity of the moment is dating whom, while wearing what on which beach. But at least I don't have to deal with one of her "friends" this evening. No need to purposely divert my eyes or turn up some music in order to drown out the sounds of perceptibly pleasurable sex. I am thankful, because, for one, I always prefer quiet tranquility, and for another, I have much more weighty things on my mind. Mainly, my thoughts are taken up by the political science conference that is about to start, for all intents and purposes, tonight, when our keynote speaker, Professor Fredrick Grange's plane should be landing at the airport.

As part of my graduate student stipend, I've been working towards putting on this conference for over a year, and I am, I admit, feeling quite stressed out about it. I really need it to go well, for my personal career and also because so many others at the University have put countless hours and energy towards it, not only the faculty and staff, but so many student volunteers. I owe it to the speakers, the participants, and the numerous helpers and supporters that this conference not only be edifying and interesting, but also offer practical paths towards helping with "Women's Advancement in Politics," the subject of the conference, and a topic I hold dear, personally and professionally. It's about time women have their say in the political arena. Having spent years researching the changes women make to their communities when empowered to do so, I am certain that our world will be a far better place once women's voices are heard and our ideas are put into action.

Even Jacqui, who could not care less about political science, is taking the weekend off from bartending, and thus renouncing the joys and rewards, both financially and sexually, to help and support me with this conference. She is a good sister, and oh so distinct from me. It always strikes me as amazing how siblings can be so different from each other. Why and how does that happen? My psychology friends tell me that this is the million dollar question, nature versus nurture. In the face of so much in common, especially for biological siblings, why do we differ from each other so dramatically?

Take Jacqui and me. Shared genetic heritage, more or less, at least same mother and father, so essentially we are made from the same human dough, but I am dark and she is light. We both have long hair all the way down to the middle of our backs, but mine is straight and brown, and hers is wavy and sandy blonde. We both have large, almond-shaped eyes, the ones that tip slightly downward, evoking a naive, melancholy look, but mine are hazel and hers are blue. Our height and the undulations of our bodies are virtually identical, yet I am considered sporty and she is considered sexy. Our personalities are equally distinct. I am two years older, so you can't say we had the *exact* same home environment; I got to know our mother a little longer before she died. I was 17 and Jacqui was 15. That makes a difference, I'm sure. As if that wasn't enough tragedy and sorrow, two years later, we lost our father to a major heart attack. My hypothesis is that he was ultimately unable to bear a life without mom and died of a broken heart. He tried though and was always such a good father. He provided for us. He was there for us, as much as he could be. I mean not in a deep emotional way, which was Jacqui's main complaint, but he was a good man. He worked hard as a public defender, helping others in need, and that's important to me. Not so much for Jacqui. She's not as reverential of dad as I am. She wanted more from him. She has always wanted more, especially from the men in her life; the more attention (and the more men) the better. Dad could never measure up. It seems like a lot of her energy goes into that pursuit. I can't imagine living that way. For me, I just hope to find one good man, one whose work and character I admire, and thus stand proudly beside, one I can learn from, one who will make me a better person through our partnership. To Jacqui, that sounds way too stale, stalwart, and old-fashioned. She often says I was born in the wrong century.

Jacqui wants a sexy hunk whom she is madly in love with and who, in turn, is madly in love with her (at least for the present moment). She wants romance, four-hour dinners of staring into each other's eyes and laughing at each other's jokes, bookended with amazing sex before and afterwards. None of these things are at the top of my list. For me, the journey is internal. I am looking for a great soul, someone who thinks with me, not some shallow rill of a man, who doesn't admire others as much as his own mirrored reflection, when love becomes some commodity, some drug of instant gratification. But such are the fears of affection and loneliness, mine not Jacqui's. I am a loner. I like to see things as they are before me. My sister would never think such thoughts, she possesses a light and dream-filled mind, and I do love her for it, and I'm so grateful she's helping me out this weekend.

***

Standing in her bedroom doorway, Jacqui cheerfully invites me in, asking, "How was your day, sweet sis?" Her easy flowing way often softens and dissipates my tendency to worry. Just her tender smile can melt away some of the tension that inhabits my shoulders and jaw.

"Lots of work, and miles to go before I sleep," I reply—a phrase she has heard me utter more than once. It's kind of my modus operandi. We all have one. I just feel there is so much to be done, and I'd like to get started as soon as possible.

"Well before you work yourself too hard," my sister continues, being very much herself, "you did promise that by the end of the week we could divvy up mom's bags, and it's Friday, so that's technically the end of the week. From here on out, it's weekend fun."

"Maybe for you. I have one of the biggest, most important weekends of my life. And there's an ice storm coming. Now, they're saying it might be a big one. I mean what are the odds of a big ice storm in late March?" I reply, throwing my hands to my head.

But seeing the childlike eagerness of her face, and knowing that it likely won't take long, I decide to temporarily put aside my anxiety over the brewing storm and my impending meeting with the famous scholar, Professor Grange, and set to opening the box of mom's handbags with Jacqui. It was amongst the boxes that we'd ferreted away for the last decade, that contained mom's things, mainly sentimental objects. We had decided together to save some of mom's boxes to open once a season, in our feeble but important attempt to prolong the ritual of going through her things. Each time, this ritual stirs up much desired memories. It is something we both seem to need. We need a lot of things, but this is something we can actually give each other and ourselves. Jacqui is often a good reminder for me of that rule: the world won't necessarily give you what you need, especially when you most wish for it. You're gonna have to do a whole lot of it yourself. I forget that more often than Jacqui does. I tend to forget about my own needs in general.

As soon as we open the box, the glee on Jacqui's face is apparent and notable. It's enough to snap me out of my melancholy illusion. With Jacqui, it's like that song "Girls Just

Want To Have Fun" is always playing in the background. It's her theme song. What's mine, I wonder? Ha, "Don't Cry For Me Argentina" just sprang to mind. Yikes. That might be a sign that I need to relax a bit more. Now, I sound like Jacqui. But seriously, Eva Peron championed labor rights and women's suffrage in Argentina. Those are causes I stand behind. She believed women belong in politics, to which I say, Amen! That's what this weekend's conference is all about: women making the differences that make a difference. Not that I have nearly the immensity or intensity of Eva Peron's passion; although Jacqui may have Eva's fashion sense.

Jacqui opens the cardboard box labeled *mom's bags* like a kid on Christmas morning. I watch as her sparkling blue eyes, rimmed with her characteristically smoldering grey charcoal eyeliner, go straight to our mother's signature Chanel bag. Jacqui examines the red quilted leather with the shiny gold-plated braided strap and the shiny gold C's in their signature embrace. It is just up Jacqui's alley, and something I would never be caught dead carrying. Jacqui looks at me, and without so much as a blink, I say, "Take it; it's totally you."

It was totally our mother as well. She loved high fashion, just like Jacqui. Dad always said that Jacqui takes after mom in her style and good humor, and I take after him in our more serious demeanor and deep-seated desire to make a positive difference on our surroundings.

"Are you sure, Ginny?"

"Absolutely. Don't think twice." I answer. "I'll take this one," and I reach for mom's oversized knitting bag.

It even has the wool and the beginnings of a scarf in it—burnt sienna and purple stripes. Maybe it was a scarf for dad? Mom did love him dearly. And she loved to knit, even though back then it wasn't a stylish thing to do. She always said it calmed her. As a young girl, I was glad when knitting, something once considered old-fashioned, came back into vogue. Not that it mattered to me; I enjoyed knitting because I could do it with mom. Plus, it busied my hands, centered my mind and also provided a useful product to give to others. I remember the day when I was 12, and Jacqui 10, and she bounded enthusiastically into my room, holding her *People* magazine (even then), exclaiming "Look Ginny, Scarlett Johansson knits too! You are actually doing something cool!" As if it made any difference to me, but it did make a difference to her, and I was pleased that Jacqui would no longer have that embarrassed and pained expression on her face every time I sat next to her in public, cradling my knitting needles on my lap.

I was glad to hold the same wool that mom had held. I would finish the scarf and wear it next winter. I breathed in the wool's essence, hoping to get a hint of mom's scent, which I missed so much. Meanwhile, Jacqui had paired her new red Chanel treasure with what she would be wearing tomorrow—a black dress that would let the red pop. My sister knows what she is doing. I smile and tell her I need to check in on Professor Grange's arrival, especially given the ice storm that is literally threatening to rain on my parade, and that tonight of all nights, I need to get a good night's sleep. Tomorrow is a big day.

***

I try reaching Professor Grange, but strangely he hasn't answered any of my calls or texts. I am relying on his keynote address to elevate the level of discourse at tomorrow's conference. While I recognize the irony of having a male as the keynote speaker discussing the furthering of women's participation in the political arena, gender equality is a fight that must be fought by men and women alike, in solidarity. In my defense, I have lined up more women speakers than men, and Professor Grange *is* one of the preeminent scholars in our field. And if I am honest with myself, I'm also more than a touch excited to meet the man whose ideas have captivated my attention for years. But more than that, I hope the conference will be edifying and will ultimately encourage change. As humans, we may be animals who can be distinctly blind to our own motivations, but we are also thinkers and we can learn to be more useful and do better.

Chapter Two

The ice is already beginning to melt and turn to slush on the walk to the University's Newcomb Hall Ballroom. I am feeling relieved at the turn in the weather; last night I could hardly sleep. I kept checking my phone over and over again for fear that Professor Grange's flight would be further delayed, canceled, or worse, that it would not be safe for him to make the drive from DC to Charlottesville on his own, that he would wreck or be stranded along the road somewhere. It seems that Professor Grange is brilliant, so much so that he stays inside his head most of the time. He can be a bit of a troglodyte, hard to reach by phone or e-mail—he told me he very rarely checks either. As inconvenient as that was for me last night, I really respect that principle. Our technology and gadgets can be so derailing. It seems that he is so focused on his intellectual pursuits that he is not really living in our shared reality. I suppose that's part of what it means to be a genius, to float a little bit above the details of the world. And that, in part, is why I cannot wait to finally meet him in person. I have read all his articles on transforming economies via female leadership, on describing methods for supporting women's empowerment in fragile states, changing policies to encourage female influence, and the huge difference that giving support specifically to women makes in terms of economic and social growth in the very places they live and need it most. His mind and ideas are fascinating.

So what that I didn't sleep all night. I probably wouldn't have anyway out of sheer nervous excitement. So what that he kind of barked at me on the phone and he didn't think to call me from the airport. He forgot to turn on his phone after the flight so I was forced to call the hotel every hour on the hour to ensure his safe arrival into Charlottesville. To be extraordinary doesn't mean that one has to be perfect in all areas. I feel lucky he made it. After all, the highway roads were probably still icy from the big storm. But the weather has warmed now and I am early in eager anticipation that all will go smoothly and well.

Before bed last night, Jacqui laid out a sharp outfit for me, and told me to unbutton my blouse one extra button. 'Live a little,' she told me. She even, without my knowing it, snipped the button away sometime last night so I couldn't clasp it high like I wanted. Now I can't even lean forward. The blouse parts all the way down to the powdery silver birthmark along my right breast. Jacqui doesn't understand. She lives in a world of alcohol and innuendo where cleavage is a commodity. I live in the world of politics, academic politics no less, and it is still largely a man's world. If you dress too provocatively, that's all anyone will see or hear. I want to make a difference, a name for myself in the process would be nice too, but that, to be sure, is secondary to good work. This conference is about ideas and potential action, how empowering women politically will change the world, not at all about low-cut blouses. I hope Professor Grange doesn't disregard me altogether.

I am supposed to greet him at Newcombe Hall at 10 am this morning and take him to brunch. I dash inside the building and check the mirror one last time. Fortunately, Jacqui showed me how to use some concealer and let me borrow her true-red lipstick.

I told her I want to look like a Washington power-broker. I don't typically wear makeup but I am thankful it is concealing my deep fatigue from the preparation work and my lack of sleep. Plus, I like the way it makes my lips feel. It's the same color Margaret Thatcher used to wear on the floor of the Parliament. No holds barred, take no prisoners red.

I sit down in the seats of the auditorium. Everything is immaculate. I finish distributing the water bottles for the various speakers. I lean back in my chair and take it all in. I practice my introduction in my head one more time. He is so distinguished and has won numerous awards in political science. The list goes on and on. He lives in Geneva now so that he can take time to research and write his next book, his magnum opus, I like to think. From his pictures he looks dashing: salt and pepper hair, sharp eyes, the consummate intellectual. I smile to myself and close my eyes. I am indeed excited to meet him.

"I'm here to see Virginia Simms," a man in a dark suit, no tie calls out to me.

"Excuse me," I lurch forward and jump to my feet, standing abruptly, awkwardly. I flatten my navy pencil skirt and almost wonder aloud if my blouse is gaping open before us. "That's me," I bumble. "I'm Virginia Simms, but you can call me Ginny."

Fredrick approaches. As he looks over the top of his glasses down at me, he arches his eyebrow and parts his lips into a soft and interested smile. He seems pleased to meet me.

He is tall and languid; his hair is a streaked hue of charcoal, but it is really his eyes that create the intensity. They overpower everything. They are fierce and steely gray. He looks remarkably dignified and timeless. Needing to break the icy gaze, I look around the room. He would be at home amidst the portraits of the great thinkers that line the walls of this auditorium, the details of his face a snapshot from another time.

He offers his hand, "Miss Simms, very nice to meet you."

I stand self-consciously before him. I suppose we will not be on a first name basis.

"Yes, finally, at last. Thank you for being here." I tuck my hair behind my ear. Jacqui insisted I wear my hair down and now in Professor Grange's piercing presence, I am wishing I had swept it away into a smart bun. At this point he seems to be staring brazenly through me. My heart is racing and my loose hair is just one more thing to manage. It's hard enough to regulate the burning flush of my cheeks. Professor Grange is undoubtedly one of my academic heroes, and now my stomach resides quite fully in my throat.

***

Thinking that I very much wanted for Dr. Grange to be well fed and happy, I had planned a quick lunch prior to the conference's 2 pm start.

"I'll have the seared halibut and she'll take the chicken paillard," he smiles across the table at me. He is clearly amused at himself. "I hear this restaurant has the best raspberry trifle in the entire state of Virginia."

I look up at him perplexed, "Excuse me?"

"Please don't tell me you are a vegetarian," he questions.

I shake my head no, "I'm just used to ordering for myself."

"Well, rest assured I've done my homework," he waves his menu ceremoniously in the air and hands it to the waitress. "Trust me, you're in good hands."

He has done his homework. Actually, he has rearranged the whole morning. The restaurant I had reserved for us was not to his liking, so instead he insisted on C&O, one of the oldest and finest restaurants in town.

A deep silence takes hold between us, and I am feeling a trace of discomfort, so I reach into my bag and pull a folder to the table.

"Here you go," I hand him his badge, KEYNOTE, it reads in bold print, with his name and representing institution encircled by the emblem of the University.

He dots his mouth with his napkin and examines the offering,

"I'll have you pin this to my blazer after lunch, if you please," his gaze rises to meet mine.

If I please?

"Um, sure thing," I respond tightly clutching my napkin in my hand.

Yes, as a matter of fact, I think I do please. His manner of speech is so proper, so erudite. I find it intriguing. This more formal style of language suits him and our environment. After all, it is quite an extravagant world we are inhabiting at the moment. The view from the glass window behind him is mesmerizing, although it is hard to notice anything at all because his presence is so very commanding.

We are sitting at a dark wooden oak table in the center of the restaurant. I prefer to be tucked away in a quiet corner with dim lighting, but this is how Professor Grange wanted it. Unlike me, he seems to like to be in the center of things. We could have been sitting by a window. There was a nice seat offered in the back of the restaurant. Doctor Grange shunned them both, asking to be positioned right in the middle of the bustling lunch crowd. He is quite particular in his wants and right now he is boring a hole straight through me with his eyes. I feel the knots tighten in my stomach. I am not used to being watched like this, and he is making me so nervous that I wonder if I will be able to eat at all. It would be so much easier for me to talk about our work than to sit here in this staring contest of sorts. Our areas of study overlap significantly. While I study political policies on female health as a way towards female equality and empowerment, he focuses more on political administration, leadership, and authority as a means to social growth. But, honestly, I am too gripped to think straight.

Quite frankly, it is mainly his eyes that are so intimidating. They are so fierce and gray, almost wolfish in their intensity. *Does he blink at all?* I wonder.

I have poured all of my passion into this world of gender and political theory. It is his world too. Ironically, he is the king of it, one of the most renowned and prominent voices, and I am voluntarily submitting myself to this lunch with him. I take a deep breath and resettle in my seat, deciding to let go of my girlish subjection and just go with it, carnivorous eyes and all.

"How is your work going on your upcoming book?" I ask tentatively.

"Exceptionally well," he offers, again not blinking, again not breaking eye contact.

He's not helping me out at all. In fact, he seems to enjoy the heightening tension between us more than just a little. Professor Grange looks a good deal older than I had anticipated, but in a handsome way, his hair more gray, his features more distinct, his gaze more discerning. The intensity is agonizing, my nerves are rattled and my hands are shaking ever so slightly. It occurs to me that he may be too smart to be an every-day conversationalist. I breathe in deeply once again. *Let's make this like an interview, draw him out*, I say to myself. I am trying to tame my inner desire to run away and hide in the library.

Thankfully, our waitress returns and disrupts the deepening gulf of silence.

"Here is the reserve wine you requested from our cellar. Sorry, it took me a while to find it. I had to get help from the manager."

He looks at the bottle with certainty and nods.

I can tell she is also nervous in his presence. Her hands shake visibly as she opens the bottle of wine. She pours a splash into his glass. He examines the color, swirls it, sniffs it, tastes it, rolls it around on his tongue. "This will be fine," he says dismissing her.

I notice that I cross my legs and turn my glance away from him to the label and then to the wine menu tucked along the edge of the table. He ordered the Chateau Pape Clement Blanc. This will be by far the finest and most expensive bottle of wine I've ever tasted.

I wasn't expecting to drink *before* the conference (or even after, not being much of a drinker at all— I'm practically a teetotaler), but clearly the expectation is that I join him. The waitress pours two generous glasses. Fredrick takes a long, slow sip. I take an even longer one.

He lifts his glass to toast: "Our greatest happiness does not depend on the conditions of life in which chance has placed us, but is always the result of a good conscience, occupation, and freedom in all just pursuits. Including and importantly wine," he smiles.

"Benjamin Franklin?" I guess.

"No, Jefferson," he leans in over the table towards me and whispers with a smile, "After all, this is Charlottesville."

I feel my cheeks flush again, this time in embarrassment. Of course. I knew that. I drop my eyes to the appetizer that now lays between us on the table.

"Of course, Jefferson," I mutter with a diffident sigh and take another long drawn out sip of wine. For the first time in my life, I really wish I could just gulp the whole glass down at once.

***

Everything is going slightly wrong. I spill a drop of wine on my cream-colored blouse and have to spend an inordinate amount of time dabbing at it at the table and then in the bathroom; the stain only highlights the blouse's low-cut nature. I look in the mirror for a long time, but I hardly recognize myself. Same long, brown hair, same pale complexion, same hazel eyes staring back at me. But there is make-up. I am wearing all the wrong clothes. My hair is wrong. I am sweating and intimidated. This man is brilliant and I can't seem to get an intelligent word out. Think of it as an interview, I say again to myself, draw him out. Men like Fredrick love to speak about themselves.

***

"What first drew you to political science?" I ask him, back at the table, summoning my best National Public Radio voice.

The man sitting across from me possesses all of the natural confidence that I lack, his speech fluent, his purpose certain.

"Political science is systematic. It studies and analyzes governance in the same way that biology assimilates knowledge through the scientific method to form explanations and predictions about the natural world. A scientist studies the laws of nature. I am a political scientist because I want to study, understand and predict the laws of power."

"Yes, but what drew you to the discipline?"

"As I just said, power," he folds his hands together.

His words land on me. This is not the answer I expected, but he says it with such definitive passion that, like some believer garnering all of the faith supplied, I sip more wine and leave my thoughts unsaid and continue forth.

"In theory or in practice?" I retort, hoping it's somewhat clever.

"Both. As Aristotle said, man is by nature a political animal. And I am very much a man."

I swallow down.

"And women?" No part of me feels at ease at this point. I am bracing with the large-eyed impression of someone ducking to avoid impact.

He pauses and smiles with enjoyment, trilling his fingers quietly on the table. The silence bares down on me. I feel the wine settling in my veins like sediment, such infelicity. Is he toying with me?

"Miss Virginia, I can tell that you are very much a woman; so you tell me..." But before he lets me, he continues on.

"You see, there are animals that are tame and animals that are wild. Some eat flesh, some eat fruits and leaves; some animals live underground, some live in trees. Bears live to be wild. They cannot really be tamed. Why do humans live, to be wild or to be tamed?"

I sidestep the innuendo.

"So political science tests this hypothesis for you, this question as to whether humans are invariably wild or tame?"

"Politics studies this question: wild or tame? And I am interested in understanding that power play."

"Did you ever consider working at a zoo then?" I set my jaw and smile.

He laughs. Thankfully. Mercifully.

"Touche," he retorts. "Political science is all about how people respond to power, how to give it, how to get it, how to dole it out."

"What about equity and equality? And striving for those?"

"You mean striving for and working towards equitable power? That's precisely what I thought you and I study and work towards. Virginia, there are good people and there are bad people." His eyes flare. "Power is the best foil for those characteristics. Political science concerns systems of power. And yes, I admit, I am a man who likes power."

My heart races. Not quite grasping his intent, I push on, "Yet it is not just any science, but a social science, and also a humanity, is it not? What about justice after all? We are biological, to be sure, but we are also, in particular, and very importantly human, and humans unlike organisms under a microscope can only be partially observed and understood."

"Justice is a good idea, if that is your concern, but it's very difficult to quantify."

"You sound like it is an idea you don't really believe in."

"I don't believe that justice is an innate part of human behavior."

"I disagree. Psychology has demonstrated through studies that babies exhibit justice."

"And what Miss Simms do you know about psychology? You study that too? I didn't know."

"My education is an evolution of things. Psychology applies to every discipline studying human beings." This guy is beginning to piss me off.

"And who's your teacher?"

"My primary mentor is Professor Patel."

He laughs.

"Professor Patel is an expert in evolutionary psychology, justice, and babies? I had no idea."

"No, he isn't. Are you?"

He pours the remainder of the wine in my glass. The wine is undoubtedly starting to make this easier and more fun.

"I do consider myself rather an expert in human actions and interactions. Humans are motivated by habit, reason, personal nature, impulse, luck, and most importantly, I reiterate, whether you agree or not, Virginia, power."

He licks his lips as he stares at me. His voice is deep and full, "Virginia, I am very pleased with our banter. It is not everyone who can hold their own at a conversation, in this way. I am duly impressed."

He says my name as if he is starting to own it.

So this was a game of conversational chess to him, one that I didn't realize we were playing, but it seems, for now, I have passed a test. I am flustered and check my watch.

"Fredrick, it is getting close to time for us to head over to the conference." I gesture to the waitress for her to bring the check. He is fascinating, arrogant, confounding and stultifying, all these things at once. This lunch did not go at all as I expected. How difficult it is to understand a mind like his, particularly with a full glass of wine.

He reaches for my hand, touches it from across the table, and releases. It is a quick movement, but to me a very bold one.

"My work is very isolating, Virginia. I don't make friends easily. But the work is so fulfilling that I don't really need them."

"I couldn't live without friends." I tell him. "And if I recall, Aristotle also said, man is by nature a social animal."

"'Tis true, but the nature of that sociality can greatly differ and power makes all the difference. Those who don't deeply understand that still have much to learn." He smiles as if he wants both the last word and to be the one to teach me.

The waitress brings the check and it sits between us on the table. I have a budget for speakers but it is nothing close to covering a bill like this one. My plan was different than the way this lunch turned out, in so many ways. I wonder if this type of extravagant meal is standard for someone so renowned in their field. Fredrick takes the check. I am not sure what to say.

I offer up tentatively, "Usually the host of the conference would pay. I don't quite have this budget, but I am happy to split the bill."

He smiles at me as if he knows he has put me in some kind of situation and he relishes it.

"I've got this. Trust me, it's my pleasure."

My cheeks flush. Is this an example of the effects of the power differentials he is so keen to study? Is this what interests him? Well one thing I do know, is that I, for one, am not interested in power plays. But on the flip side, I cannot afford a meal like this. And it was his idea, so I reluctantly let him pick up the check. I look slightly sheepish, I'm sure. This is not how my interactions with people, professional or personal, usually unfold. I really don't know what to make of it all, and now we are running late for the conference.

Chapter Three

The banquet room is crowded. I make my way to my seat and begin wringing my hands as I try to calm my heart before making my introduction. Professor Grange is once again nowhere to be found. I send one of the undergraduate volunteers to find him. In a way, it is a relief to have a break for a minute. His intelligence and intensity are overwhelming, and I am not used to the constant interrogation of his eyes and the "I could eat you up" look of his smile. It's unnerving to say the least.

The entire room is filled with excitement. The Chancellor and chairs of many departments are all here. Drs. Rome and Callow are supposed to make an appearance adding intellectual heavy weight. The seats are full. I finally see Professor Grange talking in the hallway with another PhD student—female. He is also looking intently at her. Maybe it's just his way. Maybe I shouldn't have taken it so personally.

An undergraduate volunteer gives me the thumbs up. I give the ok and the lights dim to signal all to sit. The excited voices get quieter and quieter. Precisely fifteen minutes late, the event begins. It's perfect, fashionably late for any reputable conference. Professor Grange walks into the banquet hall to impressive applause. He continues to traverse the vacillating high wire between severity and passion. He very much looks the part, although his complexion is now slightly mottled by the wine from brunch. He stands beside me and waves to the audience for them to sit.

I sweep my hair behind my shoulders as I take the podium. I shuffle my papers into place before me. I close my eyes, look down and smile as I raise my chin. My heart is racing, my legs shaking. Breathe deeply, I say to myself, and act professionally— no little girl voice here.

"Professor Grange is a world-renowned specialist in political science with a focus on the need for the greater political and economic empowerment of women as a means to real change in the world. He earned his PhD from Yale and has taught at Princeton University, and Bowdoin College. He was the Ann and Herbert W. Vaughan Fellow in the James Madison Program in American Ideals and Institutions and, most recently, the winner of the American Political Science Association's Rowman and Littlefield Award for Innovative Teaching in Political Science. We are all familiar with his plethora of academic articles in his field. He is currently working on his long-anticipated book, *Powerplay: The Failure of Democracy to Fully Empower The Other Sex*. He will be speaking on this topic today. Please give a warm welcome to a pioneer in the field and one of my personal academic heroes, Professor Fredrick Grange."

Dr. Grange delicately grazes my back with his hand as he walks behind me. There is an electricity in his touch that seems to surge through me. It's startling. *Why is he doing this?* I wonder. I falter, reminding myself that it might be my imagination. Jacqui always reminds me to keep my sensitivity in check. 'Turn off your mind,' she says. And it's true, I always seem to observe what no one else sees, and while it is a useful trait for me in academia, particularly in descriptive research, it seems fruitless in all other ways. My stomach coils into an even tighter knot. I was excited to meet Professor Grange but I did not expect it to be so tense and electric between us. I am not sure what to make of it. He stands at the podium and surveys the crowd, perched there like an elegant bird of prey. He is incisive, bold. He begins, his voice controlled and mesmerizing.

"Last week at the Hague..."

My eyes are transfixed. He is even more impressive than I realized. And his work has punch, even if it is a bit more theoretically laden than I expected. He's a heavy hitter to be sure. As he speaks, I admit my mind begins to wander, my imagination runs wild. With the wine still coursing through my veins, I feel powerless to stop these thoughts. What if he takes me under his wing? What if there could be some sort of collaboration? What if that electricity I felt works in the library... and the bedroom? I cannot believe where my fantasy takes me. It must be the high dollar wine... I should be focussed on his lecture, not sitting here pretending to listen while I'm actually thinking about having sex with him. This is so unlike me. I flush and look down. When my eyes come back into focus, I can see that he's scribbled a note and left it on the table before me. He must have done it during my brief introduction. *Miss Simms*, it reads in bold letters on the front of the fold. I tuck the note in my lap and discreetly unfold it, assuming the audience is so mesmerized by the lecture that no one is paying any attention to me.

"Celebratory drink at the end of the conference? I have a proposition for you." -Fredrick

Oh my. I touch my face. My body feels all fluttery, at once nervous and excited. Is this really happening? I want it to, but I didn't expect such boldness. What witty thing could I say in response? A proposition? What does he mean? He writes in the same odd manner in which he speaks. It sounds simultaneously both cordial and indecent. *Perhaps he feels it too*, I wonder.

Now all I can think about is what will happen after the conference. Should I go? Why not? Jacqui would. Usually I would not go out for a drink afterwards. I'd stay and clean up and get to bed. It must be the wine from lunch still humming through my veins, because I'm leaning towards it. All of my other friends would. After all, the good professor has got a *proposition*, and I'm going to take this in stride for once. He has a proposition, and I will say 'yes'. No need to overthink it this time.

I survey the audience. Suddenly, everyone stands and applauds and I realize that I have virtually missed the entire substance of his talk. I tuck the note in my purse and stand to heartily give my applause as well. His speech is over and I have barely heard a word of it. What can I possibly say of any relevance when he asks how I liked it?

"Congratulations, Professor Grange."

He steps back beside me and smiles whispering,

"Call me Fredrick. Did you get my note?"

I blush, giving myself away I'm sure, "Yes."

"And?" He grasps my hand unexpectedly. His boldness takes me aback, but I am also, yet again, impressed by it. Did he really just take my hand? Most of the men I meet, mainly graduate students, are so wishy-washy. Not Professor Grange. He seems to know what he wants. And yes, I admit, that quality is quite powerful. And while I feel self-conscious, a part of me is liking this.

He looks me up and down.

"Very nice conference. And lovely blouse. I look forward to seeing it again this evening." He smiles slyly and winks, squeezing my hand and then releasing it.

Did he really just say that to me? If he indeed meant the blouse and not me, the human being wearing it, then that's not cool. The professor may have a few things to learn too. What am I getting myself into? Just then, before I can retort, Jacqui calls to me from across the room, waving.

"Ginny! Ginny! You did it!"

It is such a relief to see her. I can feel Fredrick watching me as I walk away from him, his lips pursed, his chin raised. No need to look back, his eyes are all over me.

"Congratulations!" Jacqui hurls her arms around me. "Such an amazing success. You did great. I'm so impressed."

"My whole body was trembling behind the podium."

"I couldn't tell at all. Nobody could." Jacqui hugs my arm. "You looked radiant. I'm so proud of you. You did it!"

I smile and finally take a quick glance over my shoulder. I can feel Fredrick's gaze still on me. His intensity is almost overwhelming.

"Are you okay? You're shaking like a leaf."

"Yeah, well, I don't know."

"It's over. You did it! What is it Gigi? " Jacqui can tell when I leave things unsaid.

"Well, I'm pretty sure Dr. Grange just asked me on a date."

"The professor?" She looks around the room. "That older man who's staring at you?" Jacqui looks horrified. "No Gigi. Absolutely not! He could be our father. Shit, he's practically old enough to be a mummy."

"What?"

"You shut him down, right?"

I look down at my feet, "Umm, not really. I'm just a little bit curious. And hey, aren't you the one who is always encouraging me to go on dates?"

"Virginia, when I say I want you to date, I mean sweet guys your own age, not some old man."

She looks looks around the room again and squeezes my hand hard, "He's practically twice your age... Plus, he's so full of himself, I can barely stand it."

My whole body stiffens.

This is always the dilemma with Jacqui and me, what she finds grating and too learned, I find alluring, worldly, and actually very attractive. For me Fredrick's *proposition* wasn't creepy, it was flattering, exciting even, like the rush of pulling on the door of some great museum or cathedral and finding it open.

"Well, I told him I would meet him for a celebratory drink."

"Then, I'm coming with you."

I can see both her temper and her sisterly protectiveness flare.

Chapter Four

Fredrick is waiting for me outside the bar, looking a tad impatient. I am relieved because this time I see him before he sees me. He is wearing jeans and a blazer. He has changed, and so have I. He looks like the impeccable scholar I believe him to be, and I am enchanted. He brushes the hair out of his eyes and looks my way. Our eyes meet once again.

"This is my sister Jacqui," I stammer, feeling the same currents of electricity between us.

He reluctantly nods to her. "I've got it from here," he says to Jacqui with a half smile, and before she can reply, he turns his back to her, almost wholly blocking her out of my view. Before I can say anything, he grasps my hand and leads me into the bar to a private booth. He's not really giving Jacqui the time of day, and she is fuming.

We are in a corner booth and I feel cornered. He turns all of his attention on me. I'm not used to a man singling me out so exclusively and intensely. This is how I imagine dating used to be, just two people together, before *friends with benefits* took over. Jacqui is clearly miffed and wanders off to the bar. I wonder if part of it has to do with her being accustomed to garnering the lion's share of male attention.

Fredrick looks at me intently. "I've been thinking a lot since our lunch and in the interim have been asking around about your work in the department. It seems you are quite the overachiever, with some very interesting and innovative ideas."

My mouth is dry and I gulp down hard. How much time has he possibly had to ask about me?

"My work is isolating; a vigorous pursuit of knowledge requires it. My life is not filled with the vague purpose of so many other people's lives." He gestures around the room and looks in the direction of Jacqui. "For me, knowledge is everything, and I get the sense that you, rather uniquely, understand that."

"I thought for you, power is everything."

He smiles back at me and sets his jaw in aggravated amusement.

Jacqui is back from the bar and slides in the booth across from us.

"I'm back," she sings out with a forced cheerfulness. "What have I missed?" She has brought our three friends, Evan, Henry, and Lillian back to the table with her.

"Virginia! Bonjour ma cherie," Evan grasps my hand in his and kisses the top of it. He is always fun and charming with a light sense of humor.

"How did your trip go?" I ask, knowing he has just returned from the Basque town of Bayonne in France.

"Ah. It was very nice. The chocolate was amazing, made me think of you. Dark chocolate, our Ginny's one and only vice. Although she's so strict, she even hardly allows herself that. I brought you back some," he slides a package across the table and throws me a delectable smile. "So incredibly good to see you."

"You too Evan. And yes, you know me, all work and no play." I stash the chocolate in my purse.

I feel Fredrick cut his eyes sharply in our direction and I flush. This blushing thing has got to stop. It feels childish. I look over at Fredrick. He is glaring at us. Evan glances up at the disapproving professor and his tone changes abruptly.

"Seriously though, now I've got to integrate all of my data."

Fredrick's ears perk up, "Oh, data on what?" as if academic work is the only thing that will grab his attention.

Evan looks at him with a hint of indignation, like "who is this guy?" but politely gives an answer, "I'm working on examining the work week in France and the effects of labor laws on the people and the political climate. I suspect the research was much more fun than the writing of it will be; certainly much more delicious."

Henry interjects, "You are killing me, Evan. Conversations like these are the exact reason that I left school."

"Henry," I interject playfully.

I've known Henry for a long time and he has always been one of my favorite people. I want him to do well, but he is a classic peter pan, all fun no work. It saddened me when he quit graduate school, and since that decision he has been struggling to find himself. It's important he find a career; we are not that young after all. Henry's sister Lillian looks up, she seems more concerned with fixing her bracelet than with anything that anyone is saying.

"Ok enough about that boring stuff…" Evan looks back towards me, "More importantly, how did you feel the conference went? It seemed great to me. And Ginny, you look amazing. I have never seen you look like this."

"Like what? What are you talking about." I clasp the v-neck of my still rather low-cut dress closed, self-consciously, and press the handful of gathered fabric to my heart, regretting I asked the question. I think I know the answer.

"So... I don't know, so sexy. And you're out and about after 9 pm. What's the occasion? Don't get me wrong, I like all of it. But seriously, when was the last time you were at a bar so late? When was the last time you were at a bar at all?" He smiles sweetly.

I am mortified by his observations. Is there no sense of propriety left?

"I agreed to meet Professor Grange. He wanted to celebrate the success of the conference," I gesture my hand towards the professor. "Evan, Lillian, Henry, this is Professor Grange. Fredrick these are my friends. Evan, I believe you know Fredrick's work."

Lillian smiles sweetly.

Evan nods at him, "No, I'm not familiar, except for the talk today, but nice to meet you." Evan is visibly trying to reign in his sense of aggravation at the professor.

I look over at Fredrick. He is grinding his teeth with unrestrained impetuosity. His gaze is tense and burning. He is not happy with the situation nor with Evan's comment. I've never seen two men who have just met be so tense with each other. This jousting is all too much for me, so I decide to stand up abruptly from the table.

"What would you gentlemen like to drink?"

"I'll have a martini, stirred not shaken, thank you," Fredrick looks up at me. "Actually, make it a double."

***

When I return, my friends and Jacqui are no longer there. They have migrated to another table of students, some people I recognize but cannot place. I'm not sure if I'm pleased or upset that they have left me alone with the professor. Fredrick shifts uncomfortably in his seat. I get the feeling he doesn't really like it when the conversation turns away from him or his interests. He is the center of his own universe. I gently set his martini on the table and slide in beside him with my own glass of red wine. This time I am so tired that I just follow my instincts and gulp it down. Fredrick is utterly silent and sits there just watching me for a long time. At a certain point, I cease to notice, because the wine starts to liquify the shallows of my mind, and Fredrick rests his hand on my knee. I am starting to appreciate why people drink. He speaks softly to me, practically a whisper in my ear, "I think this place is limiting your potential. I want to speak to you about an idea I've had, a proposition, if you will."

"A what?" I have to stifle my urge to giggle.

"A proposition."

There it is, that word again.

"Indecent or decent?" I chuckle with a playful tone of dismissal. The wine has obviously taken effect. No stalemate in this round of chess.

"Both," he smiles slyly, "I hope." He puts his arm around me and pauses once again, "I want you to come with me to Geneva."

Chapter Five

Fredrick is a man who knows and gets what he wants. I lean my airplane seat back as far as it can go and close my eyes. Things are both good and bad. The conference had exceeded even my wildest expectations, everyone said so. Fredrick was so inspired by the work we are doing in my University's department and confessed to being so taken by my company, that he stayed for an extra month in Charlottesville, delaying his journey back abroad for the main purposes of reviewing my research and courting me.

We spent dawn to dusk together, touring the vineyards and historical sites. He asked me to share my dissertation in progress with him and even insisted that he bring a copy with him back to Geneva so that he might help me in this final phase of my writing. I feel incredibly lucky to have a preeminent scholar in my field reviewing my work. We spent most days together in the library and I was astounded by his work habits. I was particularly impressed by how he looked over the other dissertations in the library; very few scholars keep up with the work of the veritably "unpublished."

There is nothing trivial about Fredrick's life and work, and I felt like it made me a better scholar and person to learn from and, quite frankly, fall for him this past month. It was almost like being in the study of Jefferson himself. We worked beneath the same light in the library, my boiling brook next to his vast ocean of knowledge. We rather think alike, only his is the more expert mind. It has been such a relief to talk of ideas and principles rather than the trivialities of the gossip-corroded lives of graduate students and stars. Plus, what great company he has been. He has told me so many stories about his life. He is well travelled and very well read and liked to regale me with tales as we dined.

But Jacqui does not approve and refuses to call him my boyfriend. She keeps referring to him as *'the mummy'* instead. She likes to do a mean imitation of him stumbling into the library for his embalming. For Jacqui, the pursuit of knowledge is freedom not imprisonment. She doesn't understand the difference. She doesn't even understand her own subjugation. These "boy-toys" are using her.

The very sad thing is that Jacqui and I fought continuously until I left. I think she felt unduly threatened by Fredrick and told me over and over again how she does not like him and to be careful; she says Evan shares her views. She told me I am not seeing what is plain and in front of me. She found Fredrick narcissistic, which coming from her, is somewhat ironic if not downright amusing.

Worse, the impression was mutual. Fredrick was equally dismissive of Jacqui, which puts me square in the middle. But I think Jacqui has become blinded by her lifestyle. She doesn't understand. I told her that my life will not be subjected to her bars stool and tabloid infected opinions. From what I've seen, most of her relationships are fed by drama and sex. And half of that drama and sex takes places through the phone. Fredrick can show me the world, guide me along his exceptional intellectual path. The trivialities of life will evaporate. In the short weeks we have been together, I have already felt the effects. I want to be a student of the world, no limits, just boundlessness.

***

Admittedly, this month has been a whirlwind and now here I am on a plane to Geneva. Who would have thought it? I am taking a risk that's both exciting and scary for me. I'm not sure where it will lead. Fredrick's courtship in Charlottesville was fast-paced, constant, and exhilarating. He is a persuasive and powerful man, and so I have decided to dive into life this time rather than shy away. Geneva, here I come, but I am still so tired, and there is so much to think about, the lectures, the presentations, my dissertation, Fredrick, the dinners out, and now this. It's been difficult to sleep with so much whirling round my mind and heart.

Fredrick had tucked a letter in my mailbox before he left town. On the front of the envelope, he had written, "Virginia, OPEN ON PLANE" and had taped my plane ticket to the note. I am headed to Geneva to meet him. It all seems so romantic. Just as I had imagined in my fantasy, the intellectual journey inward with Fredrick as my tour guide, a trip across the ocean to study. Geneva was his 'proposition' at the bar. He wants me to help him with his research project, his book. It dovetails so nicely with my own work. I think I'll always remember that moment. He was looking at me with those piercing grey eyes and said, "We can be partners. Your work contributes to mine and mine to yours." His words sent a marvelous shiver straight down my spine.

This, it seems to me, is a once in a lifetime opportunity. I had previously only dreamed of this type of collaboration. My mother often said that she thought I would end up with either a priest or a professor, and honestly, Fredrick seems to be a little bit of both. I am too nervous to open the letter. I have a feeling that whatever it says, it will be further life-changing. Letters are not customary any more. They have weight. I love the look and feel of it, so old-fashioned and romantic. It even has a particular smell. Who besides Fredrick would hand write a letter?

I put on my headphones and start to open the envelope, savoring the mystery and excitement of it. Slowly I slide my index finger between the folds of the paper. Feeling the envelope tear open, my heart is racing.

The letter reads:

Dearest Virginia,

I would first like to compliment you on the exceptional conference that you put on some weeks ago. It exceeded my expectations of what an event like that could be. Your mentor, Professor Patel, had spoken with me at length before the conference about the strength of your work ethic, your determination, your intellect. I have to admit that upon first meeting you, I underestimated you. You are a woman of such great beauty that I felt it too impossible for you to be so beautiful and so highly focused and intelligent all at once. However, within the first hours of our acquaintance, I came to understand your depth of mind and the fitness of your spirit for this very special work.

Our lengthy conversations have convinced me that our minds are truly similar; our work patterns possess the same tenor and rigor. We enjoy a rare kindredness of spirit and mind that is uncommon, especially in this day and age. Your beauty and mind have captivated me. You have fully charmed me. I am a solitary man but I must admit I cannot stop thinking of you. While I have never considered this as a possibility for my life, I have found myself lonely without you. In the moments before sleep and between research sessions, I think of you and have even found myself considering the possibility of marriage. This had not been part of my life's plan until meeting you.

Such, my dear Virginia, are my feelings. This is how you've inspired me. I know some might find this sudden, but I know what I want. And why wait when you know?

If you should accept my proposal of marriage, I can offer you a grand life. You can live with me in Geneva while you finish your dissertation. We will work together to finish my book, a true union of minds and hearts. We will travel, we will write and enjoy each other. I await your arrival in Geneva with great anticipation.

Yours truly,
Fredrick

The letter falls from my fingers into my lap. Once again, this is not what I expected. Was this the proposition he had in mind all along? How quickly he knows his mind and acts. The sunset is reflecting perfectly off the waters of Lake Geneva as we make our approach to the airport. I re-wrap my coat along my shoulders as the snowy mountain peaks come into view. Time stops after I finish the letter. My heart pounds as I read and re-read it again, thinking that I must be in a dream-state from the exhaustion of travel. The flight became unbearably short, time compressed around me. I know Fredrick is about to meet me at the airport and will be anticipating my response. This is such a bold move on his part, so completely unlike the men I've met in the past who seem so uncertain and uncommitted about every potential date. These barely show up on time, if at all. Not Fredrick though. I find Fredrick's steadfastness and decisiveness refreshing and sexy. 'Our minds are kindred.' He feels it too. I am so flattered. I look out the window of the airplane and see the path before me. Both my excitement and anxiety rise in tandem. I haven't had time to think. But my heart is beating fast and hard.

An engagement, this is so sudden. Jacqui will be shocked. Everyone will be shocked. I'm the slow and measured sister. Jacqui is the impulsive one. But why not me for once. People can change, perhaps?

***

My red-eye flight lands. So this is why they call the overnight flight the "red-eye." Dang, I'm tired. I step into the cold morning air outside the airport and then what feels like straight into Fredrick's embrace. His arms are loosely around me but warm and with the glimmer of the magnificent lake and snowy peaks still humming in my mind's-eye.

He is holding my shoulders. "Welcome to Geneva."

I smile. "I'm glad I'm here."

"And....?"

"And yes!"

As soon as the words fall from my mouth, I am shocked, elated but fearful as well. What did I do? Just then his lips meet mine. His kiss is rousing and definitive and I am large-eyed and full of hopeful dreams.

Chapter Six

By the time we are in the cab, my heart has slowed to a vigorous thump. Fredrick looks down at my hand, studying our intertwining fingers.

"Please excuse me, I haven't had a moment to purchase a ring to formalize the engagement, but I also assumed you wouldn't mind. I thought it wouldn't be prudent. After all, I wasn't sure you'd accept, and moreover, these rings are such a culturally-sanctioned expense, to both the giver and the people mining them. People lose lives for the gems that wrap around others' fingers. Once upon a time, diamond rings weren't just gifts; they were, frankly, virginity insurance."

I flush all the way to the tips of my ears. While not a virgin, I do feel very inexperienced for my age. Given the times we live in, I am somewhat self-conscious about it. I re-wrap my hair into a tightly wound bun, some strands had come loose and it is my nervous habit. He rolls up the window of the cab, seemingly indifferent to the sweetness of the cool breeze and the dappling sunlight. His pragmatism cuts deep.

"No need for diamonds," I hear myself say. I had not thought of it before. I'm not really thinking, just reacting.

I lean down and retrieve my phone. I don't want Jacqui to hear second-hand, and I promised her I'd let her know when I landed safely, so I quickly text her:

"Arrived in Geneva safely. Engaged! More details to come."

Jacqui will not be pleased, but I am.

"If you don't mind, we'll stop by my office on the way back to my apartment. I have some work I need your help with."

He slides his thumb down along my hand to the base of my wrist. I suspect he is checking my pulse.

"Of course," I hear my voice respond. My phone is ringing; it's Jacqui. I turn it off.

Chapter Seven

I roll to my side and look toward the window. There is not much light coming through the dark purple curtains. As the jet lag overcomes me, I yawn and lean my head further into the pillow, partly wishing it would swallow me up. Geneva seems both large and small, grand and quaint. I learned about the Neo-Classical and Neo-Baroque styles of architecture in art history, but seeing it with my own eyes is a very different experience. It's really quite beautiful. Everything is moving so quickly through my field of vision, and my exhausted mind is trying to take it all in. The streets are lively. Well dressed, impeccably groomed people are walking everywhere. The shops are elegant. And my favorite part is how, situated amidst the classical European architecture and the marvelous medieval feel, there are so many parks and green spaces. Trees and water and blue sky sit high above and mingle with the white stone and red roofs. Jacqui would love to explore and stroll around with me. We would wander for hours, I'm certain. I hope Fredrick will roam these streets with me.

As if to read my thoughts, Fredrick interjects, "I think you understand this about me already, but I have to warn you that I am a true academic, I'm happiest with a book in hand, and I worry you may be lonely at times. In some ways, it's really too

bad a friend didn't come with you. My work is so all-consuming."
He pauses a moment and then gets out of bed, his naked body
shadowing me. "To me the work drives the passion and vice
versa. Actually, the work is my passion. I see it as the grandest
path, and in many ways, the only one I've ever travelled." His
look turns away from me to the ground. "Too much romance can
dilute and intoxicate the intellect, are you ready to head to the
library or do you want to shower first?"

It takes me a moment to register his question and answer.

"Shower, please," I turn my head and smile back at him
reluctantly. What I really want is to linger in bed, together, in each
other's arms.

Our sex had more thirst than passion. It was not the kind of
sex that consumes you, the flowery kind I'd read about in novels.
Perhaps Fredrick's mind is just far too controlled for that. First we
toured his apartment. We knelt on the floor together, spending
long stretches examining his collection of books, Aristotle's
Politics, Plato's *The Republic*, *On Liberty*, *A Theory of Justice*, *The
Prince*. It was all there, the grand path laid out before me, and then
he looked at his watch and took my hand and led me into his
room. It was the one room we hadn't toured. My heartbeat
surged.

"Do you want me to close the curtains?" he had asked as he
stepped past me towards the window.

"Half-way, please." My mouth was so dry I could barely
speak.

His room was dimly lit by the pulse of the city.

"Ginny," he said without hesitation folding back the covers of
the bed, pausing and looking at me for a long time. "I want to
make you come."

My breath caught in my throat. No one had ever spoken to me
like that. It was an abrupt transition from curtains to coming. He

turned back around and leaned into me. I wriggled my toes in my shoes, closed my eyes, and bit my lip, taking several steps back to the wall, a slightly awkward first dance. Then without speaking, his eyes still fixed on me, he undressed me in the same matter-of-course way in which he approached the world. His cheeks were flushed red with restraint as he unclasped my bra and then drew my panties down to the floor. I could feel his warm, wavering breath move down along my thigh. Fredrick was a master of self-discipline, but I could tell he was very aroused and was trying hard to muster his restraint and control. There seemed to be nothing trivial about his life, his art to walk most fully within the bounds of decorum. I twisted with girlish delight as his breath followed its path back up the length of my leg, sweet torture.

"Be still," he stated, standing once again.

But instead of listening, I lifted my chin and gave my mouth to his, a challenge. I instinctually needed to fill the precise and mathematical silence of the moment with some playfulness.

"Yes, please," I breathed into the kiss. "I *do* want you to make me come."

He smiled and breathed the same "yes" back to me.

"Show me," I said with the airy tone of voluntary submission.

This time without decorum, his lips were once again forceful and decisive, and there was no wine in my veins to dilute the intensity of the moment. I could feel my heart quicken as I unbuttoned his pants and let the fabric slip through my fingers to the floor. He stepped forward, his erection now substantial and free. I heard myself let out a gasp.

"Now sit back," he lay me down on the bed and parted my legs.

He gazed with his usual intensity, but multiplied by a million. He traced his finger along my gentle folds, almost examining me, and I could tell he could not stop.

"We start here," his voice cantered delicately. "Beautiful. And it's all for me," he declared, pressing his head between my legs, his tongue trilling up and down my hollow spaces. His was a thirst too, even his tongue felt hard.

I gasped at the overwhelming sensation of it all, and upon hearing the pitch of my voice, he lifted his head to watch me writhe, moving his fingers to where his mouth had been, so that he could feel me and move me and watch the expression upon my face at the same time. His eyes were as piercing as ever, expressing a particular satisfaction. He touched me once again with his fingers, "So wet," he murmured, "Good. As it should be." He lifted his hand to his face and licked his fingers, groaning. "I can't wait to take you, Ginny."

I was speechless. This was happening. His eyes were searing with the impatience of desire as he opened my legs further and penetrated me. I gasped as I felt him crash into me; I could feel his pleasure upon entry, and mine in return. I felt the pulse and heat of his erection inside of me. It was so intense. To let another inside you. To wrap yourself around another. I drew him closer, holding his back with my hands. I needed to hold on. I wanted him to be still a moment. To rest with me, inside me.

He grasped my hands and pinned them above my head. His whole body pressed down on me, undulating. He started to move in and out, first slow then faster and faster. It was forceful and brisk, sharp and stimulating. His eyes were closed.

"You're mine," he said, breathless, repeating it, seemingly getting off on both the thought and sensation; the former fueling the latter.

I could hardly move, pinned, but felt a coiling deep inside of me. The quicker he moved, the more I breathed in the perfume of all of our pheromones now conspiring. While I noticed my mind's distractions, observing what our bodies were doing, my body was also responding in ways I never knew were possible. I could feel his hardness inside of me and a pulling from some unknown place, and where they met, a folding and unfolding, like waves crashing over and over. The sensation was building and building and finally blurred my thoughts. My hands bound above my head, and with great wanting I kissed him once again, needing to feel tender lips, and suddenly our bodies seemed to splinter with sensation and pleasure, first him, rippling, then me, then a prolonged silence. My eyes fluttered as I watched the shadows dance along the ceiling.

"I came so hard," he said releasing my hands and rolling over, "you did too." He kissed me briskly on the lips, got up, and walked out of the room, declaring, "I could make a habit out of that."

As I lay in bed dazed and looking around his room, I noticed a small dry erase board hung along the back of the door, "*We are what we repeatedly do. Excellence, then, is not an act, but a habit - Aristotle.*"

Chapter Eight

I knew Fredrick didn't waste time with trivialities, but it wasn't quite the reception I had expected. A proposal of marriage, a kiss at the airport, a trip to the office, sex, and now back to the library. It left me with feelings of closeness and sensuality, followed too closely by a certain detachment, and now here we are amidst the stacks. But after all, this is the life I seem to have chosen. Academia can be that way, both enlivening and isolating.

"It's just the jet lag catching up with me," I tell Fredrick, buying myself some time, when he asks from across the library table if I'm okay. I am looking at the books, but not opening them, and I'm struggling to find a work rhythm.

He glances at me over the rim of his glasses looking stern and concerned.

"Let the work invigorate you. Please. Like in Charlottesville. It's important."

After roaming the stacks, I find my way back to my seat at the table. Fredrick has been pouring over my dissertation ever since I gave it to him and now is no exception. I love the library but not immediately after making love. I really just wanted to fall asleep. But my mind is too worn out to process these impressions, and my stomach is twisting and turning in a way that feels disconcerting. I am hoping that I'm just hungry.

"What time is dinner?" I yawn again, think he might take the hint.

"I'm not sure yet. It will depend how my interviews go."

"Interviews?" I look at the clock. It's already 4:30 pm.

"I was hoping to," I run my hand up along his thigh, "have some more of your time."

"Ginny," he gives me a sideways look, "you have to learn to tame these desires. The work needs to come first."

"But…" I feel like a scolded school girl.

"If you really can't focus, then I can have Ben take you back to the apartment."

"Ben? Who's Ben?"

"Ben Warren. He's my research assistant, at least in name," Fredrick shakes his head dismissively. "He is far too concerned with the art and whimsy of Geneva and utterly lacks determination and application. You need habit to work. Even if nothing comes of it, you just have to do it. Ben is a man full of youthful illusions and vague purpose. His assistance and research have been lackluster to say the least; he will never get anywhere." Fredrick look up at me briefly, "But I suppose he can take you back to the apartment if need be. His sense of geographic direction is about all he has going for him, if you ask me."

I want to say "I didn't ask you," because I've always had a deep-seated aversion to people speaking negatively about others and I'm also pretty insulted that he rebuffed my playful advances, but I hold my tongue. Fredrick points across the library to a man with his back turned to us. Ben is sitting at another table across the room; books are piled all around him and he repeatedly flips a pencil through the blonde curls of his hair. He is wearing jeans and a soft looking, casual t-shirt. I watch him and breath a sigh of relief. Can someone look kind from the back?

***

As I wake up in Fredrick's apartment, I think how nice it would be to stretch my legs, to step out and feel the morning. I am alone in the bed and venture into the living area. I find Fredrick reading on the couch. I'm not sure how long he has been there, but imagine it's been some time. I thought we would make love last night after dinner, but Fredrick didn't initiate and I was still exhausted from the flight.

"Any chance you might like to go for a morning run or walk with me?

"Not a very good one."

I breathe deep and offer again, "Perhaps the fresh air and exercise would do you good."

He finally looks up from his book, "What will really do me good is finishing this book. Now that will be a breath of fresh air."

He doesn't seem to be *finishing* a project at the moment. He is just reading on the couch. But I guess it's all part and parcel of the bigger process.

I push it a little, "Maybe it will go more smoothly if you take some time away from it, put some balance in your life."

"Maybe it will go more smoothly if I'm allowed to focus."

I am stunned by his contempt. I've never been spoken to like this before. I don't even know where to put myself. I stand there, quiet, feeling stung by the surprise and disappointment that courses through me.

I look around Fredrick's apartment. It is dim and rather melancholy, and I think how getting flowers might in order for today, but then I think that maybe I should take things as they are, his reclusive mind might need it this way. I decide to play some music; that often lifts my spirits. A little quiet piano, some nocturnes. I have heard Fredrick say he is fond of classical.

"Can you turn that down?" he practically barks.

Intense to the good and the bad, this is going to be quite an adjustment. Although he says he is a fan, I haven't actually heard him listen to music, have never once heard him put it on. Hurt, I decide to turn it off completely and walk out the door announcing that I'm going for a morning walk.

"Oh good. Have fun," he replies, without really looking up from his book.

Chapter Nine

Later that evening, we tuck into a small restaurant on Rue du
Prince. I am starving and queasy at the same time. Fredrick keeps
using the term helpful when he talks about me over the phone. I
notice that he doesn't hold my hand. Instead, he clutches my
elbow and steers me left or right past the tables. It feels like a
pinching sensation. It was a bit the same way with the sex this
week, very efficient and directed.

"I like it when you wear your hair down," he says as he sits
down across from me. He seems restless, possibly annoyed even.

I reach back and unclip my hair, letting it fall down around
my shoulders. He seems pleased, aroused. He licks his lips and
turns his attention to the menu. He is a man with very particular
tastes.

The restaurant is small with dark mahogany trim, rose-tinted,
floral wallpaper, and small, intimate tables. There is a step down
as you enter and no windows, only flickering candles. I can smell
the leather from the soft, antique chairs. The restaurant oozes
romance from every dim corner, and yet somehow here with
Fredrick, the whole setting is making me feel a little bit out of
place. Our waitress, Lara, she tells us, slides up beside the table
and hands Fredrick the wine list. He doesn't look at her or even

acknowledge her, but eventually settles on a Sancerre. I smile and thank her, apologetically overcompensating for Fredrick's lack of personal engagement. Fredrick doesn't seem to notice my interaction with Lara. He also does not seem to be in the mood to talk, so I look around the room until my eyes settle on a couple sitting in the far back corner. They are totally engrossed in one another. The man's hand keeps cupping her face and brushing the hair away from her eyes. They kiss at the table. I find it difficult to look away. They seem the perfect juxtaposition and foil to our table. My experience with Fredrick, at the moment, is nothing like that, no tenderness, no care, only intensity and direction. Perhaps it is just the might of his mind, his intense journey of self-perfection that makes him so focused but also so distant. I remember my mother once telling me about love, "If you want to be with someone extraordinary, you have to be willing to put up with someone extraordinary." Perhaps this is what she meant.

"Wine, Ginny?" Fredrick interrupts my thoughts as the waitress returns.

I pull my eyes away from the couple in love. He just kissed a crumb of pie away from the corner of her mouth. I am reminded of the film I loved so much growing up, *The Princess Bride*. In it the narrator speaks of a rating of kisses being a very difficult thing, but the formula, he states, includes "affection times purity times intensity times duration," something like that. This couple had all the above in that kiss. I want to experience what that kiss feels like. I look towards Fredrick.

"Yes, please," I reply startled and admittedly somewhat flushed. I smile back at him then at Lara as she fills my glass.

She reminds me of Jacqui, blond waves and playful dark rimmed eyes. My heart sinks low and aches for my sister.

I look up at Fredrick. He has pulled some papers onto the table from his bag. I stare at him. He sighs and scratches his chin.

"Ginny..." he seems almost annoyed. "There are are some significant gaps in the data here. Pieces are missing, making the argument unconvincing if not inconclusive."

He points to the paper on the table and I realize that he is reading my dissertation. I am hurt and confused, first that he is so absorbed in my work rather than me, the woman right here in front of him, and second that he is being so critical. It doesn't make sense to me on so many levels. For a moment I feel very childish, the phrase, "I just want to go home," rings through my head. Instead, I steel myself and retort,

"Really, I haven't received that feedback before. In fact, Dr. Patel and I have reviewed this several times and he indicated the exact opposite. He felt like the work was drowning in data. He told me the data was bogging me down almost like I was over-arguing. He said the evidence is clearly there and I don't need to belabor it quite so much. Kind of a 'she doth protest too much.' How interesting that you both have such different views."

I take a deep steadying breath. I am literally digging my heels into the ground. I feel like caving in but I don't.

Fredrick's eyes close and his jaw sets. Silence, punishing silence.

"Are you mad? You seem angry," I respond.

He closes his eyes again as if restraining some thought or action.

I look around the restaurant nervously. The lovely couple in the corner has left, so there is no place for my eyes to retreat to, no fantasy world to linger on.

"Does Dr. Patel's opinion matter to you more than mine?"

I flush, "Well, I wouldn't say that, but he is a leader in the field and I've been working with him for years now. I respect him *and* he really knows my work."

"Need I remind you that I am also a leader in the field, more so than Patel." Fredrick glares at me. "And your fiance," his eyes are searing.

Waves of sensation travel up and down my back. His pupils are dilated, undressing me. This is his game, I think to myself. Debating like this is his passion. It turns him on. I test my theory and unbutton my blouse one more button, leaning forward towards the table. His neck flushes with color. *So this is how you like it*, I think.

The waitress interrupts my slow strip-tease seduction, reappearing carrying two plates.

"But I didn't order." I say perplexed.

"I ordered for you," he responds. "When you lost your focus a while back, staring off into space. I figured it would be the most efficient and I know what's good." He is licking his lips again.

I drink down my second generous glass of wine and look to my plate in silence. His moods are so mercurial. I can't keep up. I decide to make a move.

"Speaking of our engagement," I begin in a timorous tone, "I was wondering something today."

"Yes?"

"I was wondering, why did you court my affection?"

"Did I? I thought you courted me?"

This verbal banter is exhausting. I stare back at him licking some sauce from my thumb. His neck flushes red again. Ok, now I've got his attention.

"You are serious? Ok Ginny, let's see…well you are very beautiful, and sexy in the way that I particularly like, and you are very smart. I saw you as dedicated but not overly ambitious, which as you may have surmised—in a woman is not attractive to me and I know would not suit my lifestyle. You seemed to admire me. And honestly Ginny, don't take this the wrong way.."

As soon as he utters that phrase, I brace myself. When people say that, I know they are going to say something hurtful.

"But it seemed time that I take a companion. When I met you, the thought occurred to me that you would make a good wife. Traveling and studying and writing can be lonely. And you seemed up to the task to help me in both. Lord knows Ben is of no use in either department, companionship or work."

Fredrick continued in a vein that seemed quite strange to me. "I was very happy you said yes—to the drink after the conference, to coming to Geneva, to my rather sudden proposal. I thought it was all a good idea."

I notice he says "thought" but do not interrupt him.

"I haven't had the happiest life, Ginny. My parents divorced early, my mother was a quiet but needy woman. She wanted me by her side as she read, but had few other passions. I did not play much, and wasn't with other children. Our home was more like a library. It was not a happy go lucky childhood. But it's what I got used to, it's what I know. I thought if I was very successful academically, showed her I had what she seemed to respect, the ability to write these books she always carried with her, then she would be happy. But it has not been the case. She still sits in her living room, unhappy, reading and alone. And it's been nose to the grindstone for me my whole life. And that's okay. It is how it is. I hate to say it, but I'd hoped our union, yours and mine, Ginny, would bring me more joy and less trouble than it actually has. You're quite a bit needier than I expected."

Check. Now he's hurt me. The silence of things left said and unsaid takes hold between us.

"Excuse me," Fredrick rises abruptly from the table bumping the waitress and knocking one plate down along his pants.

"Sir, please!" the waitress blurts. "Oh no! I'm so sorry." She frowns.

I jump up from the table with my napkin and wipe the food from his lap.

Fredrick's face reddens with anger, "I fully expect our dinner to come from your paycheck... and my dry-cleaning bill," he spurts with indignation.

"Sir, it was your own fault. You stood up and knocked me back."

"I would think as a server you should know better than to just stand there."

"You don't have to be so disagreeable," the waitress opines, and I am secretly very pleased that she does.

"The only thing disagreeable here is your opinion..."

Our waitress is as speechless as I am. She cleans up in silence and walks away. She is visibly annoyed and I am dumbfounded. I also do not know what to say.

I had no idea he could be so cold, so captious. I can feel the sediment of the last week settling around me. Our eyes meet in a peculiar way.

"Wait, you research gender equality and the empowerment of women. How could you say that?"

"I didn't say she shouldn't be working, she should just be better at her job," he casts a glance up me and then down me and nods his head indicating that these assumptions are about me as much as the waitress. It's all so castigating.

We wait in silence for the manager to come settle the bill. Fredrick is quiet, his eyes stormy. There is too much to say and neither of us can figure out how to say it.

"Can we walk back to the apartment?" I murmur embarrassed by the whole scene. "I could use the fresh air."

"Fine," Fredrick reluctantly shakes his head. "But please eat a few bites more of your dinner. You have been losing weight since you've been in Geneva, and that is not part of the plan." He looks at me warily. "Look Ginny, I don't want to fight with you." He offers me his hand. I smile back at him and squeeze his hand. The chess match is seemingly at a stalemate, for now, and I am relieved.

***

As we walk out of the restaurant into the street, he grasps my elbow once again. We walk, soaking in the silence of the night. As we cross the first intersection he pauses a second looking around, and then abruptly he pulls me into an alley. He grasps my face, backing me into the shadows and against a brick wall. He licks his lips looking up and down the back street.

"You are looking very sexy," he presses his substantial erection against me. He smells my hair and grasps it, pulling it back and up into a ponytail, tipping my chin to the sky. His eyes are devouring me, his tongue takes possession of my mouth. I am the focus of all of his intensity and passion for the moment as he lifts the edges of my skirt and unzips his pants.

"Turn around," he says and twirls me so that I am facing the wall of the building. My hands find the cold bricks for stability. In spite of myself, I feel my back arch, lifting my behind towards him. He pulls my panties to the side and enters me. I can feel the heat of his erection inside of me, all of the emotion and intensity of dinner pulsing between us. He moves in and out of me, slowly at first. He reaches around me and fingers my clitoris with crazy-making concentric circles, swirling around in the front, as I am taken over from behind. It is all so overwhelming and confusing. This is not what I imagined, but once again my body is overcome with sensation. I can feel all of his focus and desire as he kisses my neck, one hand on my clitoris, the other cupping my breast, as he thrusts in and out of me. My knees are shaking as I instinctively match his rhythm. I reach around and grab hold of his hips. My whole body quickens to his.

"Ginny...I'm sorry," he says for both nothing in particular and everything at once, but something about the way he says it allows me to end the fight and yield to the moment and with that surrender, I explode with pleasure in a dark alley in Geneva.

Chapter Ten

I wake up from my deep sleep hoping that somehow my circumstances might be different, but they are not. Once again Fredrick is not around to answer my questions. I am beginning to understand how dependent my own happiness is on his actions or inactions. This now all-too well-established pattern of resolute submission of my desires to his is not working for me. Fuck this! I pick up my phone and dial my sister.

"Ginny! Is everything okay?" Jacqui's concerned voice echoes out through the phone.

I hear laughter in the background. She is clearly in the middle of something fun. I immediately burst into tears, a seeping tide of redness overtaking my eyes.

"No, nothing is ok," I say.

"I knew it! What has that creep done to you, Ginny?"

"It's just that nothing is as I thought it would be. Not the work, not the connection, nothing."

"Come home!" she demands.

Just the sound of her voice rejuvenates me. My native strength of will is returning to me.

"I can't. It's complicated, and I have to finish my dissertation. That was part of the point, but it's like he's hijacked it."

"Okay then, finish your dissertation, quickly, and come home." Her kind and loving voice reverberates in my ear from across the ocean.

***

I slide my bag along the library table and sit down beside him. I pull out my computer. It has been weeks now since my plane landed in Geneva. Fredrick is in a constant state of agitation, and my dissertation is held hostage by his continued review of it. I am waiting for his 'expert' feedback, but day by day, week by week, time is just passing. He has clearly been awake all night and his mood is unsteady. He wags his finger at the air to indicate 'just a minute' and I wander through the tall shelves of the library in search of some feeling less heavy than the one that clings so tightly, deep in the pit of my stomach. Newton, Einstein, Galileo, all of these minds were mercurial and difficult. *It is part of the package*, I tell myself as I trace my finger along the spines of the books.

I peer through the gaps between the shelves. A man walks up to our table to greet Fredrick. I spy through the cracks in the books; Fredrick doesn't look up as the young man speaks. Well, at least it's not just me who gets that treatment. But in a way, that makes it worse. Doesn't that make it *him*? Me, I can at least work on. Me, I have some control over, although lately I feel so much less of that; my internal control is feeling dimmed and diminished, taxed by the day.

The man has a notably boyish look. Somehow, he is masculine, boyish, and an old-soul all at once, wrapped in a soft-looking t-shirt. Something about the breadth of his shoulders makes it hard for me to look away. I can tell it's Ben, Fredrick's research assistant, the one he has spoken of so dismissively, over and over again. I can barely see them through the towering books, but I detect that the few words Fredrick speaks to Ben have cut him. Ben shakes his head and turns and walks away. I notice Ben's honey colored curls, the way the light falls like liquid through them.

"Ginny," Fredrick calls out. He is tapping his pen impatiently on the table. "This work is so convoluted. I am going to need at least another week with it. I recommend you find some fun things to do."

I literally hang my head and grab my bag, heading back out into the streets of Geneva alone again. He won't let me look at his manuscript, and until he finishes his review of my work, my hands are tied. The other night he tried to tie my hands to the bed. I refused. Then I would have been doubly bound, no thanks. I decide to find a tour book and really see the city.

Chapter Eleven

Seeking solace in history, I venture to the old part of the city to spend the entire day within the weathered old stone walls of the St. Pierre Cathedral. Seated on a hill in the center of Old Town, the church is both minimalist and stunning. To think, 850 years of that view, the lake, the city, and the mountains. I find myself rather unconsciously braiding my hair down the side of my neck. Having taken in the gothic paintings and pondered the centuries of souls who sat in the wooden pews, I wonder what to do with myself next. I am looking around at the other people and notice the bold form of a man. Unlike everyone else around him, he is not looking at the carved wooden chair reputedly sat in by Calvin himself. Rather with his back to the chair, he is carefully, quietly, observing a stream of light, a ray of sunshine streaming in from the window. He watches the lambent dust particles coruscate and flutter by him like magic. His wavy blonde locks look angelic and luminous in the light. He puts his hand out as if to gather the light spun particles. He seems mesmerized, and in turn, I find myself hypnotized by his boy-like wonder and spontaneity. *Fredrick would never do that*, I think to myself, shaking my head. *He only cares about questions of the intellect and power.*

Just then the man looks up. Wait, I know him. It's Ben, Fredrick's research assistant. His blue-green eyes liquify with delight. We nod at each other in recognition and our eyes seem to catch onto each other. He looks at me with a generous, warm, kind smile, and I feel seen for the first time in a long time. As our eyes are locked, I feel my face flush and time stands still in the sunlight. I don't know how long this lasts, it seems like a long time, much too long for two people who barely know each other to look into each other's eyes. But for no apparent reason, I scamper to the other room and tuck myself behind a wall. My heart is racing. I feel like such a fool. I am an adult woman, and I am hiding. I lean my back into the steady, cool stone wall of the cathedral. I close my eyes and try to compose myself and calm my body. I will just wait here until he leaves. That's what I'll do.

My heart rate surges again as I hear Ben talking with his friend walking in my direction. He is speaking in not much more than a whispered hush, but loudly enough for me to catch upon his voice and words. There is something about his voice that resonates straight to my heart. He doesn't realize I can hear him.

I think, although I can't be certain, that he says to his friend, "That woman we saw, I think she might be the most perfect woman I've ever seen."

The whole room is spinning. I tell myself that he must have been speaking about someone else.

Chapter Twelve

I am back in Fredrick's apartment. It's his, not ours. That is clear. I haven't even fully unpacked my bags, a symbol that a part of me is not fully here. For once, I'm grateful to open the door knowing that Fredrick won't be there. I'll have plenty of time alone should I need it. I do need it. I collapse on the couch. I feel like I've just been struck by lightning, every limb tingling, or perhaps by a truck. Things hurt.

Fredrick never comes back to the apartment until after dark, not even to change for dinner. I just meet him in some prearranged restaurant. He is typically late. I am sad and sensing that Fredrick feels I am getting in the way of his work. I must say, to feel *both* distressed and distressing to someone else is quite new to me and very uncomfortable. I don't like this new combination at all. I am not a fan. This is supposed to be a happy time, not just a vacation, but an engagement journey. Something is clearly not right.

I feel a tear appear and then another. As I rest on the couch letting my tears fall freely, the image of *Madeline's* Miss Clavel in her nun's suit running through the dormitory, crying, "Something is not right" runs on a loop in my head. Growing up, Jacqui sometimes called me Miss Clavel. She still does when I fret over something she's done or is about to do. And it's true, "Nobody knew quite so well, how to frighten Miss. Clavel" as Jacqui did for me. I can feel it. Something is amiss. But this time it's not with Jacqui; it's definitely me.

The tears roll down at a quickened pace. I truly feel a grievance, but what is it? Fredrick is handsome, at least to me, and very smart. What's wrong with me that I can't appreciate him now? In Charlottesville, he swept me off my feet. He is precisely the kind of man I've always *said* I want to be with. He is someone I can really learn from. He is top in his field, *our* field. I mean, get real. I knew he had work to do in Geneva. I just thought there would be a place for me here. At the very least, that I could work on my thesis. At least we could have lunch together. Or that we could share in his work. It doesn't feel right. I feel shut out. Is it because it's Geneva, and I am far away from home, from Jacqui? But I'm a big girl. I've always prided myself on picking myself up by my bootstraps when needed. And Geneva is beautiful. Isn't everyone at peace in Switzerland? Isn't that the point of Switzerland?

I make myself tea and grab the box of Petit Suisse cookies that have become my surrogate friends. They melt away in my mouth one by one. The tea is so soothing. I'm not used to focusing on my own troubles like this. Even when my parents passed away, at the very worst time of my life, my focus turned to Jacqui and what I could do to possibly help her get through it and feel better.

Maybe that's it. Maybe I feel too useless here? I'm not at my best unless I am helping others and have a purpose. How many times have I scoffed at the idea of women weeping over romance? How many times have I said, "She just needs to leave her pity party and get out and volunteer or find good work?" Meaningful work is the key to happiness. It's probably time to listen to my own advice.

But things are changing like the clouds, so is Fredrick's mood. He is lusty and then distant, my own thoughts and feelings for Fredrick, my desire and admiration for him, metamorphize by the day, by the hour.

Maybe after Geneva, when he's done working on this particular book, we'll be okay. I'll feel that reverence and admiration again. He'll let me have my life back. I am typically so circumspect, so prudent, why did I impetuously say yes to his hasty proposal and to such a controlling man?

"What are you in control of?" I hear my mother's voice in my head.

My thesis, I think. I pull my computer out of my work bag, and for the first time in weeks, I find solace.

Chapter Thirteen

Feeling better after accomplishing something, I bring Fredrick an afternoon espresso to the library, as I do sometimes, and spy Ben sitting on the library's front steps. I decide to brush away the strange encounter in the cathedral and approach him with a vigorous smile.

"Hi Ben!" I call out with heightened color and affection. "I'm Ginny. I feel like we haven't formally met yet. I just came to bring Fredrick a coffee."

"How very dutiful and thoughtful of you. But Fredrick went for a walk, so I get to take a break." Ben's smile seems to have a touch of the mischievous.

"Really—a walk? That seems so unlike Fredrick."

"He is a mysterious man."

"I guess so," I smile though I am also grating my teeth. "He never takes walks with me," I say.

Did I really just say that out loud? What's wrong with me?

"Well then, he is a fool," Ben says with equal gravity and levity.

"Excuse me?"

"A fool." His expression nearly levels me. Our gaze meets, his eyes are a supernal blue, with a golden ring around the iris.

Looking into them, some dark haze that was residing inside me seems to clear.

"Would you like this espresso?" I offer it forward towards him, that spinning feeling begins to overtake me once again, the sensation that made me hide in the cathedral.

"Why don't you have it?"

"I've had mine. But thank you. Take it and we can walk, you and me." The words come out of my mouth before I can restrain them.

"Well," he says taking the cup, "then it turns out I am doubly indebted to Fredrick's foolishness. Thank you. Much obliged." He looks into my eyes as he speaks. It melts me.

As we walk and talk, I become taken with how conscious we seem to be of each other's presence, and particularly of how Ben listens and takes up my words. Lately, it seems that Fredrick hears my speech as if it's all been said before, like it's nothing fresh or new to his worn ears. But Ben seems to glean more from what I say than I had even realized I was saying.

I stumble on the sidewalk and he catches me. He seems to never lose sight of me somehow. I feel a tingling sensation where he touched me. I look in his eyes. It's like a light turned on in him. I feel my cheeks burn and wonder what color pink they have turned.

"Want to grab a bite to eat?"

My heart surges. Since our encounter in St. Pierre Cathedral, I have found myself startling awake in the night and have felt a certain hunger for his voice and even his touch.

"I'd love to, but I'm here to help. I am looking up some things for Fredrick."

"Ginny, you are neither his secretary or assistant; that's my job, unfortunately for me."

"How's that going for you by the way?" I playfully but guiltily ask, regretting the words as soon as they are released. I'm not sure I want to hear the answer to that question.

"Well, to tell the truth, it ain't easy. He's not the easiest guy to work for, to say the least."

All of a sudden, and without thinking I blurt out, "Well he says the same about you."

Ben's eyes flash, "So you've had a conversation about me with Fredrick." He pauses for a second, "What else has he said then?"

I stumble over my language, "He has complained that you don't work hard enough."

I witness the words wash over Ben, but he steadies his countenance in a good natured way, "Well, I have to say, he doesn't really let me; he really doesn't like anyone looking over his shoulder or even really knowing what he is working on. It's pretty strange; I don't get it and I've given it plenty of thought. I suspect it's insecurity about the nature of his own work and ability, but who am I to say?"

I feel embarrassed by my words and let down my guard. In actuality, I find this line of conversation most interesting. I agree with Ben. Fredrick has a very strange relationship with his work, and I just don't get it either. Ben and I sit in the silence of a somewhat shared reality, the kind that brings two people closer together in their attempt to make sense of it. I look up at his face. His short, loose, luminous golden curls surround his lovely countenance. His eyes are languid and easy as the sky, freckles sprinkle his face, haphazard and joyful. I feel like I am surfacing from something. There is none of the gravity and hopeless petulance of Fredrick between us.

"Well I think you are someone to say. You've been working with him a long time."

Ben screws his mouth into a ball, indicating it was the stupidest thing he's heard. "Yes, unfortunately, I have. Maybe no one has explained to him what a graduate research assistant is and how much we get paid!"

Hearing this makes me angry, and I am now taken aback by how much I want to protect Ben. He is completely correct, research assistants don't usually do this much work for the petty stipend they get. Fredrick is too good a person to exploit someone, and for heaven's sake, amongst other things, we study equity and worker exploitation.

As we come to the end of our walk, and we circle back to the library, Ben stops, leans in, and quiets his voice,

"I was hoping I might see you today."

I can feel myself blushing. I don't know what to say. As he had been talking about his life on our walk, I paid attention to his words but had also been distracted by his distinct physical charm. At times he has a defiant look, something about the way he petulantly tilts his chin up to the sky. It is as if he knows or thinks others are looking at him, and he almost embarrassedly is going to keep going in spite of it. He looks particularly boyish at those times, like I can see him doing that exact same gesture as a ten year old. Then he softens again. And the twinkle comes back to his eyes.

We stand there on the street, needing to separate but neither of us moving. It's as if time has stopped, the pulse of the city and the day slowing to a near stand-still. We feel something in each other here in the silence, a blind urge that rises up. And for a moment, I want to just kiss him and completely forget about my troubles.

Ben speaks at last; thank goodness, "Well thank you for the walk and talk, and the espresso. You made my day."

I finally made someone's day. Ben pauses, stammering over his words, like he has something else he wants to say, "Are you okay, Ginny? I mean, it seems like you've been losing so much weight since you first got here."

I look at him, stunned, first that he's noticed, and second that he would bring it up. "Yeah, it's just…" I hesitate.

He continues, "Look I don't mean to make you uncomfortable. I understand. It's just, well…watching you and Fredrick… " Ben looks around grasping for words, like he doesn't know how to say it, "Just take care of yourself, please."

What has he seen? I have a hunch but I don't quite understand. I stare back blankly at him and my stomach tightens. Ben shakes his head, "Anyway, tell Fredrick, I'll be back in a minute. I've got to get a bite to eat. I think the coffee is making me jittery. At least I think that's what's doing it."

He closes his eyes for a fleeting instant.

As I walk back into the library, my inward troubles overcome me. Finding Fredrick back in his usual spot, I swallow back my tears and summons a smile. Feelings beget feelings after all; I'd like this to be a pleasant encounter. We could use one. Fredrick seems to see me and immediately puts a book on top of the article he is reading. His response is characteristically unwelcoming, but also quite strange, almost as if he is hiding something. It takes him a long time to look up at me. Maybe I should ask more questions than I do about his whereabouts. At this point I've learned to read these signs; he is deep in his work and displeased with how it is going. He is frustrated and it will be projected onto me if I stick around.

"Do you need something, darling?"

That's another thing, Fredrick seems to unconsciously add "darling" in the weirdest way at the end of a sentence just when he wants to scold or say something nasty, but instead it's as if he consciously decides to be patient and polite. And it comes out *so* wrong. It doesn't even sound like Fredrick when he says that word, '*darling*'. It sounds like he is borrowing the endearment from someone else; it's almost in a different accent, for crying out loud.

"I have a question," I say, desperate to stop the tears welling up in me. "You know that research assistants make very little stipends right? And most people have them work in accordance with what they make. I've noticed you have Ben working around the clock, and it just doesn't seem right to me. Maybe you don't realize what he makes?"

Fredrick pauses and gives me an icy stare.

"*Darling*, this is not the first time, but it should be the last, that you try and tell me how to do my work. I will not take dictation from you, Ben, or anyone, and I do not appreciate the attempt. I certainly don't like you meddling in my financial affairs. And I especially dislike the idea of him, of all people, talking to you at all. That boy never ceases to annoy me. Don't let him influence you Ginny; his influence is less than useless. Besides, if he doesn't want to be a research assistant then he should finish his dissertation and get on with things. It's his choice to live as he does. I sure as hell wouldn't do it."

Clearly, my words have shaken him. Clenching my teeth for solace and strength, I begin to wonder if this fear of others' criticisms lies at Fredrick's very core. If it's what's driving him.

I decide to continue in this vein, "You want me to stay clear of not just Ben, but everyone. We've been here a while and yet I haven't really met any of your friends or even colleagues. Maybe we could invite someone over for dinner, or go out with some people sometime?"

Fredrick looks angry and then takes a moment, and for an instant I think he is actually considering it.

"That sounds awful. I'm so tired by the end of my work day that the last thing I want to do is then work at conversation with people who don't have much to say."

"But don't you want to get to know people? Doesn't it feel lonely, just us all the time?"

And honestly, I think to myself, it's mainly just me by myself and for him, it's pretty much just him. So I, for one, could really use some company and new blood.

"Actually, that suits me fine. Work, and then you and me." He does not bring up another topic. The least he could do is change the subject. My sentiment is just hanging in the air, first awkward, then like it never even happened.

I gather my things and leave quickly. I've been doing a lot of fast exits lately. This engagement is a sham, a placeholder.

Chapter Fourteen

It's a beautiful day, weather wise, but I'm just not feeling it. Sleep evaded me last night. 3:30 am has not been my friend. I decide to call Jacqui and thankfully she picks up. I imagine her turning to a half naked man, who is smiling up at her, while she comments coyly, "Sorry handsome, but it's my sister." And I remember that for all her boy craziness, that drove me mad, I have and always will turn to her first, and I will always be her priority. For this I am most grateful.

She answers with her characteristic upbeat, "Hey girl!"

"Hey," I respond, and she is immediately onto me.

"What's wrong? You sound awful."

"Oh, it's ok…"

But she is not buying it and interrupts me saying, "Spill girl. This is me. Don't leave anything out."

"Well, I'm just feeling really alone." I take a deep breath and decide to just vent, rather unlike tight-lipped me, but I can do no other. "Fredrick invited me here, which I thought was very romantic, and the proposal was just what I thought I wanted, but now Jacqui, he works from breakfast until dinner; he doesn't even find time to eat lunch with me. And you know what, honestly…"

The tears are gushing forth, "I probably wouldn't care so much, if he would just take my hand when we walk, instead of walking five steps ahead of me. I'm always looking at his back. He never reaches out to touch me, and when he does it feels, I don't know, insensitive, wooden. And his gaze. Jacqui, he doesn't even look at me anymore. It's like he sees right through me. I feel like I'm invisible. I don't think he notices anything about me. I feel like I sound so shallow and petty. I never thought I needed *this* kind of attention."

"Everyone needs *that* kind of attention, Ginny. It's called love. And when you are in love, you notice everything. Because you really care. And you want nothing more than to spend time with each other, gazing at each other. You could and want to look at each other all day. It's not being needy Ginny. It's being in love."

"And when he does touch me, he's so controlling."

"Controlling? What do you mean?"

She's onto me and not letting go. I don't even have enough experience to find the words for it.

"With sex, with all things, he likes to be in control."

"Like how?"

"He covers my eyes, holds my wrists," I confess.

"There's nothing inherently wrong with that, but how is that for you?"

"Sometimes sexy, sometimes scary, but always overwhelming."

Jacqui is silent for a long time.

"Honestly, Gigi, I hate that this is your experience right now. It takes a lot of trust to do that stuff… and it's certainly not to be done with mummified control freaks!"

I hear her and continue, thankful to just be able to speak, "And it's not just me he wants to control Jacqui. His comments about others are so harsh. The way he talks about colleagues' work. It's embarrassing; as if his work towers above theirs. You know what—it doesn't. And his tone *with me*. What happened to the sonorous voice and twinkle in the eye? I mean really? Half the time, he sounds downright mad at me when he talks to me, actually angry. It's me, Jacqui. No one gets mad at me. What's up with that?"

Jacqui was right there with me, and dared to respond honestly, "All good signs of a real jerk if you ask me. All telling. And it will only get worse Gigi. These things only get worse. Cut it off now. Be done. Come home."

I do want to just go home, so badly that I can't even give that an immediate response. Maybe he really is just a big jerk. Then again, Jacqui can be such a black and white thinker. Over the years, I've alternately been supremely frustrated by and admired her characteristic decisiveness. It certainly can make for much easier decision making. Jacqui would pack her bags today.

Regardless of the content, it feels so good just to tell someone else these ruminations that have held me captive. A feeling of relief washes over me as I allow myself to vent a little more. "For example, yesterday at dinner I asked him to hand me the salt. I had to ask *three* times. When he finally did, our eyes didn't even meet. He never even looked up. His contempt is palpable. Am I doing something wrong? Just when I think he is bound to show attention or even say something interesting or complimentary, he doesn't."

"No big surprise there," I could hear the simmer of Jacqui's sarcastic laugh.

"Jacqui, this is serious."

"I know sis. It's very serious. And it's much too soon for you to feel like this; way too soon. You're in the honeymoon phase, though thankfully *not* the actual honeymoon. Although this is way too close to it for my comfort. It doesn't sound sweet at all. It should be honey, Ginny, sweet as honey. This should be glorious. You should be the world to him and vice versa."

"I don't need to be the world to him, but at least a continent. Heck, I'd take feeling like one vast ocean he wants to explore. What do I do about this?"

"I say come the fuck home. But knowing your tempered self, you would tell me to not make any rash decisions—although I think it's fine if you do—but you would tell me to clear my head. Usually about now you would go running."

She has a point. She's right. For now, I'll run it off.

Chapter Fifteen

Listening to Jacqui's advice (my how the tables have turned), I don my running clothes and set out to run by the lake. This usually helps. I really need to stop brooding. Despondency never helps anything. There's just too much inward focus going on with me; it's like my mood is covering everything with a gray haze.

As I am running by the lake, the magnificence of the mountains in the distance seems to shrink out of reach, much like the companionship I contemplated so hopefully on the plane out here. I thought Fredrick and I would be working side by side, learning from each other, a communion of minds that would in turn enrich our hearts and bodies as well. But he seems to be going it alone, wanting to do so, sitting alone amongst the stacks. Why?

In my fantasy, even when I wasn't with him, I'd be walking around going about my business with a special tenderness, looking forward to seeing him later. But I don't. It's nothing like I imagined. I both long to see him, in large part from loneliness, but also almost dread seeing him, worried that things will feel wrong when I do. Such disenchantment all around, a pervasive withering. Life feels smaller with this union.

As I look around the lake, I start to think of all the people who probably feel like this. All these people, walking around living unhappy lives. That's not me. That doesn't need to be me. This is madness. What's preventing me from stopping this in its tracks?

As I run, my lungs fill with fresh air. I take in the green trees, the lovely looming Alps a reminder of nearby France and all the hope that other places hold. The landscape is all so natural, so real and easy. The scenery seems in stark contrast to my relationship with Fredrick, which feels so forced and difficult. I tell myself to focus on the beautiful terrain and the breath. Let go of the questions and let nature take over.

I find my breath and my stride and finally release the thoughts until I'm in my body, in a meditative state. There is a figure lying in the grass, reading a book, his body so relaxed, so comfortably in himself. He seems engrossed, his energy sensual and engaged yet very much at ease. Now *that* is how to be with oneself, alone with a work of art and enjoying the company of nature. I find his energy drawing me to look in his direction. He rolls over onto his back, slowly and gracefully as I approach nearer. I do a double take. Is that Ben?

Shoot. What do I do now? Do I run past? Should I stop? He is Fredrick's assistant after all, and it has become pretty clear that Fredrick is jealous already. But maybe talking with Ben will get me out of this state of self-absorption. Maybe I should focus on someone else for a moment. Lord knows I could use some human contact. I really hope he can't tell I've been crying. But it's been a while now since the tears flowed.

I should just keep going. I decide to keep running; it's more in line with my modus operandi. When in doubt, don't. But just then I hear the graceful figure call out to me, "Ginny," and I know I'm caught.

I run up to him on the grass. He seems shy, even a bit diffident and nervous. I smile, attempting to put him at ease. He looks at me quizzically.

"Everything ok?" He asks.

I'm taken aback. Can he see the sorrow in my face? Is that why he is more quiet than usual? Could he be gauging my emotional state? I try to smile harder.

"Of course. My face is just flushed from the run. And you? How are you faring?"

He looks at me. He's not buying it one bit.

"Faring? Oh, yes, quite well thank you." He laughs at what I guess is my rather Victorian speech. I can almost hear Jacqui's laugh echoed in his.

"I always like how you speak," he says, to ensure I take it as a compliment, with a gentle tone. "What are you up to today?"

It seems like he wants to hang out. Someone wants to hang out with me! I feel like the kid on the school ground getting picked first for foursquare or kickball. Our eyes lock. After what feels like ages of a hushed silence, when I can't take it anymore, with only the wind and birds as our soundtrack, I break his celestial blue-eyed gaze and look down, at once not wanting to alter the intense bond our eyes are creating and yet wondering once again if this is altogether appropriate. As I look down, I take in his worn blue jeans, baggy and yet fitting each muscle perfectly. His pretty bare feet, and as I look back up, eye his comfy pale orange t-shirt with the Buddha-like figure gracing his chest that looks so soft to touch. It reminds me of the warm setting sun.

"What are you up to?" he asks.

"This" I say, pointing to my running attire, not giving him much to work with. "You?"

"This" he says pointing to his book. I take in the author. George Eliot. Interesting.

"Good?"

"Only the best," he replies. I know enough about literature to know it's a classic, and I find myself wondering about his heart and soul. He seems gentle. He exudes an energy that is so different from what I have been experiencing of late. There is something so caring in his face and even in his bodily stance, something strong and protective but also sweet. He goes on, "That is, if human dynamics and emotions concern you, and I don't mean so much politically, as I know they do, and that's in this book too, but in terms of individuals, how they love and suffer and interact. I highly recommend it."

I take a moment to ponder what he is saying. Individuals matter. It's not just about power and politics for him.

As I sit with Ben on the grass, it strikes me how incredibly agreeable he is. He is at ease in his own body. Even the way he is relaxing now on the grass, his legs splayed out in front of him, barefoot, his t-shirt untucked, he is very comfortable in his own skin. He leans back on his arms and lets the sunshine wash over him.

"So it's just you and your sister?"

"Yes. My father passed away soon after my mother died of breast cancer. That was years ago."

"I'm so sorry."

"Yeah, she fought it for over ten years. It was the aggressive kind, so it came back with a vengeance. I don't actually have any memories of my mother before her cancer diagnosis."

His eyes soften. I desperately want to change the subject. I just don't want to cry. This feels like it should be my moment to be happy.

"What about you?" I ask.

"It's also just me and my sister. My parents were much older when they had me. They died when I was a teenager."

"Then you must have spent a lot of time caring for yourself."

"Yes, and my sister too. She is younger. She struggles and I know she misses me. It's hard to be away from her." His jaw clenches as he speaks the words out loud. Boy, do I know what he means.

"But to come this far with your studies and have no family support."

"Well, yeah," he says in a silly, faux British accent. "It all works out well enough, doesn't it?"

Even though he is speaking of serious matters, when he talks about himself it is in a light-hearted tone, without the heavy and grave importance that so many others—Fredrick for example—add to their own weight. It turns out that Ben has accomplished far more than Fredrick gives him credit for. Ben earned scholarships all the way through college and garnered academic and athletic awards in high school that lead to his University acceptance. He was top of his class and accepted to graduate school with full stipend and the research assistantship that landed him at Fredrick's door. He has always worked jobs that paid his way, nothing luxurious he added, but he's happy he made it on his own. He revealed all this in response to my questions, without any haughtiness, just the facts.

Ben is light in both step and speech and I'm finding it very refreshing. I could use more of this—this is what I've been missing. Is this what we are always searching for, that very essence or thing which we feel we are lacking?

We sit and talk for a while longer, "So how is Geneva treating you?" he asks.

"Fine." But then I pause and realize that Ben is asking earnestly, and now is my chance to be myself and open up. He is asking me to show myself to him. If I don't, I am undermining his offering. And it is too sweet an offering not to open that door.

"Well, actually. It's been a bit lonely. Fredrick usually works until at least 7:00 most evenings, I don't really see him from breakfast until then—save for my coffee delivery, as you know.

But tonight he says he needs to work even later—to catch up on things. It's just not what I expected. I guess that's what they say. Sorrow comes from being attached to certain expectations. I guess maybe I need to change mine."

Ben falls silent. He looks almost shocked and saddened. The corners of his admittedly beautiful mouth turn down. He seems lost in thought, intently staring at me. I can't figure out what he is thinking. And now I'm starting to feel self-conscious. Was I too bold in revealing my discontent? Some people don't like that. He finally speaks.

"Why is Fredrick working so much? I thought you two were also vacationing here?"

"Ha. Me too. Funny that. Anyway, it's fine. People need to work. It's good for us humans. Without meaningful work, what is life?"

He is visibly taken aback by my words.

"Ginny, what is life? What is life?...It is love."

Our eyes meet. I pause, my breath falters as I take in what he has said and then reply, "Well I meant without meaningful work *and* love." I look down at my hands once again.

"Ginny, yes it's true, but make no mistake about which one of those comes first."

I fall silent. He has uttered just a few words, but I am truly taken aback. I feel chills all over. I wonder if he can possibly notice the goose bumps that have instantly made an appearance on my body. Is he right? Work has always come first for me. What if I've been completely missing the boat all these years?

"Fredrick's going to be working so late tonight. Perhaps you could join me for dinner?"

"Sounds perfect." His whole face lights up.

Chapter Sixteen

I make my way into Café Papon, pleased to see the wine glasses on the table; it's as if each glass has been patiently waiting for me all day. And in turn, I feel I've been waiting for them. I've never craved that end of the day glass of wine with dinner, but have now grown accustomed to it in Geneva.

Just based on habit, I assume that I'll be the first to arrive for dinner, as is routine these days. But as I look around the dining room, I spot a handsome figure. I know from his back, his blonde waves, his broad shoulders, and his bodily ease, that it is Ben. He turns around just then and finds me standing still and looking at him. He smiles. My whole being at once relaxes and opens. He waves me over, smiling all the more. In front of him is a bottle of wine.

"Hi. So good to see you. I hope it's ok, I ordered a bottle of wine." I read the label: Chateau Beau-Site Saint-Estephe Cru Bourgeois. "I've been letting it open and breathe; I think it's ready. May I pour you a glass?"

Did he really come early to order and let the wine breathe? How thoughtful. What a glorious gesture, what a generous expenditure of his time for the benefit of my pleasure. In turn, I feel like I am relaxing and opening up for the first time in ages.

"Yes, please. And thank you kindly."

He smiles again. Each smile opens me more to him.

And look, he changed for dinner. He is wearing a crisp shirt, white with dark blue checks, it looks ironed, and yes, I look down, grey wool dress pants. He looks so handsome. I've only seen him in his jeans and t-shirts, which trust me, are incredibly delectable in themselves. But this, well, this takes it to a whole new level. This man has style. I didn't think I cared about such things. But looking at the very handsome figure he is cutting, I can't deny the appeal. I take my seat and I think I must have the biggest smile in the restaurant. And for once, I am thankful that Fredrick is working late as usual.

Ben holds my gaze as I sit and pours me a glass. "So, you too did a lot to take care of yourself growing up," his gaze is soft and beckoning.

"Yeah, I did. There were a lot of hospital visits and I learned to wait a lot. Wait, for appointments, wait for test results. Lots and lots of waiting."

"So what did you do to pass the time?"

I chuckle to myself.

"If you seriously want to know," I laugh out loud. "I learned to repair watches."

"Really."

"Yes, really."

"Watches?"

I hold out my arm and point to my mother's antique silver watch that hangs like a bracelet from my arm.

"I got into it because my mom's was always broken and it was something concrete that I could do to help her. It was something that I could hold and touch and that I was in control of. I needed to control time in some way. And it was something I could fix. It was the perfect outward expression of my inward desire. And it's the one adornment that's completely practical and needed."

"And then?"

"And then it became an obsession. I apprenticed, I studied books, I would go to antique stores and buy old watches and deconstruct them and rebuild them. It's sort of a passion of mine."

"And here you are in Switzerland, watchmaking paradise," he smiles.

"I guess it's true," I laugh. "I've been so stressed out that it honestly had not even occurred to me." But of course, Rolex, Omega, Patek Philippe.

"Well, you have to go to the Jardin Anglais. It is the most famous clock in Geneva. It's down by the lake."

"Really, how so?"

"It is a clock made of flowers."

My soul leaps at the thought. Clocks and flowers, two of my favorite things.

All of a sudden, Ben's look turns from lovestruck to dumbstruck. What's happened? I follow his gaze and see that Fredrick has entered the restaurant. I hadn't noticed him but he is standing near the hostess, his look upon seeing us is palpably annoyed. I had texted him that in his absence I was going to dinner with Ben and where he could join us if he finished up early—I felt it the prudent thing to do so that he didn't feel left in the dark. But truth be told, *most* of the time, Fredrick does not get my texts, he doesn't check them or something. And he certainly doesn't seem to read or mind them. Interesting and unlucky that he paid attention to this one.

Fredrick seems to be moving in slow motion. It's painful. When he finally gets to the table, he sits down beside me, and I feel an angry energy emanating from him. On the best of days, I am aware that his presence has the unfortunate effect of making me self-conscious and uncomfortable, as if at any moment when I say something he will take offense, and then verbalize it, embarrassing me. But with Ben here, that feeling seems magnified and intolerable to manage. Maybe it is better that we don't go out with company after all.

"Hello. How was your day?" I attempt to normalize, harmonize and bring Fredrick into our fold. He's not having it.

"Busy. There is never enough time in the day. Do you feel that Ben?" he asks, snarkily.

"Nope. I don't. I mean *some* days are busy of course, but in others, I find myself pleasantly enjoying each minute, savoring each one."

Ben's words go straight to my core, knowing that he is speaking about moments such as ours today.

Fredrick starts to speak about finding a flaw in a colleague's weak argument. In excessive detail, he tells us what's wrong with the data and how it doesn't add up to the author's claim. I continue to drink the delicious wine. Fredrick then lists for Ben what he wants him to do tomorrow regarding the book. Ben respectfully listens taking it in, but I can tell Ben finds it inappropriate and downright rude. These are after-hours and there is good wine on the table. Why should we speak of work?

Fresh-baked bread comes to the table and the aroma makes me happy. I'm hungry and the wine is going right where it should be. I ask Fredrick to please pass the olive oil plate which is sitting on his side of the table, so I can dip my bread and keep the wine a little more at bay. Fredrick doesn't seem to hear me, or doesn't acknowledge that he does and continues detailing what he wants Ben to do in the library tomorrow. While seemingly listening to Fredrick, Ben leans over and picks up the dainty dish of oil and hands it to me. He looks me straight in the eyes, and a feathery flutter rises and falls up and down the midline of my body.

"Thank you," I say and smile. I decide to let the wine take me wherever I wish to go.

As Fredrick drones on, holding court, Ben looks at me sweetly. I wonder if Fredrick can see the admiring look on Ben's face, if he notices? Then I feel Ben's leg gently nudge me under the table. It rests, gently touching my leg. I wonder if it is an accident. I wonder if I should move mine. Not knowing, not really needing to know, I remain very still. Enjoying the amplifying warmth of his touch, under the table, I do not pull away.

Fredrick drones on about our colleague's research. I make a concerted effort to join the conversation, diffuse the aggression, and temper the critical tone, hoping we can move on. I venture, "Well not all arguments are flawless. And that's ok. I think there is sometimes room for questions and uncertainty."

Fredrick impatiently barks at me, "It's not ok. It's not ok at all. What's the point? It doesn't surprise me, given your work, that you'd take such a stance."

Did he really just say that? Who says things like that? He is no longer speaking with polite condescension, just pure contempt. My face flushes. I feel hurt and am not sure what to do. I feel my eyes give a beseeching look towards Fredrick—please stop. Not here, not now. But he pays me no mind. He has no discernment.

I look towards Ben, immediately self-conscious. I feel caught in the questions of this moment. What if right now Ben is asking himself, what kind of woman chooses to be with such a man? What level of passion and self-esteem could there possibly be inherent to someone who has agreed to marry Fredrick Grange?

I feel my décolletage, which is a bit more exposed than usual tonight, flush, and I look up, almost afraid to see Ben's response to Fredrick's openly hostile remark. My heart is beating a racing staccato, and I feel like I am sinking. There is such hardness in Fredrick's voice, in his unresponsive ways. I am fully saturated with the haze of emotions that surround me. I would cry but no tears surface. I feel like a deer in Fredrick's inhuman headlight.

And just when I feel the dizzying panic of my desolation flare up, I notice the warmth of some touch. Ben's leg is touching mine again, soothingly, as he gives Fredrick a look of comic disgust. It is as if Ben doesn't know whether to laugh or scold. I can tell he would like to say damaging things to Fredrick—even more than perhaps he usually does. I stare into Fredrick's face but find zero recognition of the reaction he is getting from Ben. Fredrick continues to talk. He doesn't care at all, and somehow in my blind naivety, I am amazed. Another chess match.

I look back at Ben wondering what his next move will be. And then I see it: faced with the decision to derisively laugh or scorn, Ben simply smiles a smile that somehow simultaneously holds both within it, and more. What an ingenious smile; it showed such good humor, such empathy, and a wisdom held in lightness. How did he pull that one off?

And then as Fredrick studies the food on his plate, Ben turns his gaze towards me. His smile is filled with understanding. It immediately warms and soothes my entire being so much so that I smile back at him. Ben's expression seems to automatically react to mine and he takes it up one more notch, his whole being is lit up. I see him. He sees me. Ben is both a man and boy at the same time. At once very protective yet playful. It is not what I thought I wanted and needed, but it is real, and easy, and natural. How much I would rather be with this man, sitting across from me, than the man beside me.

My musings are interrupted by Fredrick's sharply anointed tone.

"Ginny…" he seems even more annoyed. "We should talk about some of these significant gaps I am finding in your data.

They can't just be ignored." He sounds as though he is speaking at me from up high on a pulpit. And I think to myself, hell yes they can. Especially now. That is if they even exist at all.

He points to the paper and I realize once again that he is reading my dissertation. He seems to take it everywhere with him, and now he is using it as a weapon against me. It would be one thing if he were talking about my wrinkled dress or my illegible handwriting, but this work is a huge part of me, the culmination of *years* of work and thought. I look at Ben and flush from the wine and the deep embarrassment I now feel. I want desperately to crawl beneath the table. Ben smiles back at me sweetly and reassuringly. I am struck by the gentle disposition of his eyes. It is a quality that speaks to me and stirs me. It is a language that I don't fully understand.

Fredrick throws my dissertation down on the table with an excess of drama and flair, a lawyer attempting to stir a jury. I look down at the napkin resting in my lap. The breathlessness around the table is tense. Ben clears his throat audibly and reaches for the papers.

"Fredrick, I couldn't disagree more. I think you are wrong. Ginny's work is beyond excellent, and you know it." Ben says forcefully, his brow furrowed. I have not heard this tone from his lips before. The softness in his eyes has all but evaporated.

Fredrick closes his eyes and sets his jaw. There is more than a sparse remnant of malice within the contours of his face. Again, what was once veiled contempt, is now in full view for all to see and it is not a pretty sight.

"Ben, I'm not sure whose idea it was for you to be at this table in the first place, but certainly you must realize that this is none of your business. Please keep your unhelpful and unwelcome opinions to yourself. You have as big an aversion to deep thought as anyone I have ever encountered in academia. Your self-indulgence is your hallmark. Poor Ginny needs neither your help nor your opinions."

The air is crackling between them, and Fredrick shakes his head from side to side in a way that indicates disgust mixed with vain delight. I look between them and see them as they are for a flickering instant. My predicament is vast.

"But why?" I respond angrily. This is just too much. "Ben is here because I invited him to dinner. In fact, the only one who was not going to be at this table was you. You, if you recall, had to work late yet *again*. And speaking of work, Ben read my dissertation; why can't I hear what he thinks?" I turn to Ben. "I want very much to hear your opinion."

"You can't because I say so."

The silence falls over us like a veil, hushing the air around us.

"Well, you do not have final say in the matters of my life."

Fredrick closes his eyes again as if restraining some thought or action.

I look around the restaurant nervously. My loneliness sinks in and it shrinks me. The restaurant feels smaller, the walls and ceiling nearer, the noises caustic and singeing. The reassuring warmth of Ben's leg has fallen away.

"Does Ben's opinion matter to you?"

"Of course it does. You're not the only scholar here."

"Is that what you call yourself? A scholar." His words are searing. "From what I've seen of your work thus far, I am beginning to wonder. Your work, Ginny, has holes all the way through, and Ben, I'd likely have something to say about your work if you actually ever *produced* any."

Fredrick glares at me with a meanness of spirit that is almost unbearable. His face wears the look of contempt, pinched and crinkled at every corner. I feel it all pass through me, a cold wind.

Then, all of a sudden, there it is again. My dark companion, that overwhelming dolor mixed with anger like a fever on top of a hot temper, and this time as it surges up, there is nothing I can do. I jump up from the table clumsily knocking over my wine. It spreads across the cloth with great permanence. I gasp and then retreat past the waitress, past the hostess, past the entrance and spill out onto the dimly lit avenue. I am running once again. I am not sure where I am going. My dress is stained too, with the wine and now my tears. They are in full bloom, cutting across my cheek. I stop for a moment and take my sandals into my hand. I keep my head down, rushing past people and running as fast and as far as I can. I run until I can't run any more.

Chapter Seventeen

I stop when I reach the shore of Lake Geneva. Its beauty, a gift on this dark night. Fredrick had promised over and over again to bring me here but never has. And now he never will. Here I am, my toes soaked in her cold waters, my heart racing. The queen herself, Lake Geneva. She is lit up by the moon, shining like a jewel, the mountains floating behind her like a crown, uncommonly dangerous and stunning. I look around. I am surrounded by grass and spring flowers in the moonlight. There are benches and crisscrossing paths. This must be a park.

Jardin Anglais. Ben had spoken of it to me earlier at dinner—during a tender moment that seems so very long ago. It is one of his favorite places. He told me how it held a clock made of flowers that I need to see. Tears are still flowing involuntarily and I need them to stop. I need something new to occupy my mind, and so I wander into the vast darkness of the meticulous grounds to find the clock.

I feel like I am walking through a painting, no detail spared. Ben and I spoke about the clock, but the park is vaguely labyrinthian in the dark like this. Maybe with time I can understand the landscape. Time. Wasn't it Benjamin Franklin who said that lost time is never found again? I have wasted so much time trying to please Fredrick and figure him out. But I am here now, and the park is lovely. It is traditional with trees huddled and majestic. The fountains are elegant and unhurried. I round the corner and see an embankment decorated in a circle of flowers. It is just as eccentric and beautiful as Ben suggested it would be. How charming, a clock made of flowers, *L'horloge fleurie*. The numbers are perfectly shaped by all the petals. The second hand is in constant motion. The swift motion of the hand came at me loudly.

So much has happened in so little time. This man I thought I knew now regards me with such aggravated indifference. So much was said, but so much was left unsaid, and I wonder that in running from the restaurant, I have just filled in the ellipsis.

"Oh, Ginny, I hope you will be happy," Jacqui had said to me before I left. Her words now reverberate around me. She was right. I should never have come here. This city is so unfamiliar. All of its beauty is lost on me, imprisoned by my own false expectations. How could I be so naive? All these beautiful sights now spoiled by the aching loneliness that cloaks me. There is nothing that reminds me of home. I sit down on the grass in front of the clock and curl my knees to my face. My emotions are loud and unavoidable. I am forced to succumb.

Fredrick would hate me even more for this. To him, this would be some melancholy illusion, some weakness, more added proof of my neediness. However, the emotions are too abundant and my life and my work come crashing down around me all at once. I idolized Fredrick to the point of blindness. It's all my fault. How foolish to be so naive. Finally, I totally give in; my pride evaporates and I surrender. I can no longer hide my deep fear and grief. The tears bloom once again. This time I do not run away, I sit where I am and just let them take root and let the emotions wash over me. The tears flow fully, foraging a trail down my cheek, along my collarbone, along and down my breast, over my silvery birthmark. They form a miniature pool in that tensile yet flimsy cloth that drapes along my knees. I have far too many questions.

Chapter Eighteen

I'm not sure how long I have been sitting by the flower clock before I feel the presence of another person. It's that heightened sensitivity that is the disadvantage of deep loneliness. And even with all of the vigilance, I feel wrecked and unable to move. I am desperately hoping that this person won't notice me here. A shuddering breath goes through my entire body and I bury my head even further into my knees in the hopes of fully disappearing. How could I wade so deeply into Fredrick's shallow soul? He is not even half fond of me. And to think that I have spent so much time in the last few months stifling every part of me, acting more like a piece of furniture, not wanting to draw his ire and judgment. "Ginny, don't let your emotions overtake you," he would say, and so for weeks my eyes remained dry, save for the handful of tears I narrowly allowed to flow.

I feel the uneasy sweeping steps of someone slowly approaching. I turn my pallid and frustrated face toward the sound.

"Ginny?" a voice calls out; it sounds smooth as a meadow.

Startled, I look up again. Who could know me here, in this city, in this state of deterioration? Who could even care? It's

certainly not Fredrick. I strain my swollen eyes and see Ben
walking towards me in the moonlight. He is a stirring sight.

"Ben?" comes forth from the deepest fibers of me.

What is he doing here? I feel excited, sad and embarrassed all
at once. I am not used to feeling vulnerable and certainly not used
to someone coming to look for me when I'm sad, let alone finding
me. My face must look horrible, swollen and abused by the
intensity of the last hour. He walks over to me. He is holding
something in his hand. It is a bottle, the wine from dinner. He sets
it on the grass beside me and sits down.

"It's me," he says playfully.

"I'm sorry," I say and look down.

"What for?"

"That's not how I anticipated dinner going. I'm sorry for the
fight and sorry that I ran out. I'm just generally sorry."

He pulls out a handkerchief and hands it to me. His hand is
soft; the clean and pressed handkerchief even softer.

"There's nothing to be sorry for. I'm glad you ran out.
Fredrick was so unkind to you. He deserved what you gave him
and more. I can't believe that he insinuated there was a problem
with your dissertation. It is flawless and brilliant. Fredrick only
wishes that his work was half as rich as yours. That's why he's
been pouring over it for so many weeks. He's jealous. Fredrick has
no original thoughts, and he is a fool to treat you that way. He has
no idea. To have you and take you so for granted… it's insane,
it's…." his voice trails off, a red flush of anger mixed with wanting
desire creeps up his neck.

I just stare at him. He offers me a sip of wine and I take it. I
must have misheard him. My head is throbbing with the irritation
of the heavy, deep sobs. How did he know I was here? He reaches
over and touches a strand of my hair that has fallen free. He
caresses the tendril with greater care and focus than Fredrick has

even once shown me. I am struck by the look in his eye, the question and tenderness and wonder. He is rapt.

"Fredrick is a narcissistic and selfish man, and selfish people never think about the needs of others; he deserved some push back," he says with blind indignation.

I look at him and feel an instantaneous pang of something deep inside of me. His voice is like a trickling stream, an idyll.

"I'm sorry," he says as he releases the tendril, seeming to scold himself. "Can I take you home?" He offers.

His eyes meet mine. There is something both exquisite and effortless there.

"Yes, but first," I pause wiping the moist tears from my face, "Can you just hold me for me a moment?" I can't believe I have said that out loud and in that way. It sounded like the voice of another. I am as startled to hear those words pour forth as he is.

"Please," he says in a half-soothing and half-beseeching tone.

I look up at him and I see in his eyes the flicker of some unknown emotion, it's an intensity that is so beautiful that it is painful, and so I fall forward into his lap. This is what it means to succumb. He wraps his arms around me and holds me close. His warmth and the beating of his heart soothes me.

After what seems like a long time, he speaks, "Ginny, let me take you home."

I shake my head no, desperately and fervently.

We are alone, a desire crackling between us. And as quickly as the wind can shift, the tension heightens. I can barely breath. I can feel his heart racing beneath his shirt. His blue eyes are blazing and dilated. I wet my lips looking at him anew. His eyes are so layered and loving. I can tell he is trying to understand me. He is listening and seeing me. I see his lips, soft and pursed with concern. I want to kiss him, and I notice that he too has almost stopped breathing. I want to close my eyes but I cannot. I am stuck in this unnamed emotion, unable to look away. *Desire*, this must be what it feels like to hold in love and heat.

"I can't..." I start to say, as I arch my back lifting my mouth to his. It is more a reflex than a decision. I have to do it. I feel that I have no choice. He brings his hand to my face, his thumb grazing my cheekbone. He is kissing me back. My mouth opens and our tongues find space to move and explore. I've never been kissed like this, so smooth and wet and warm. He playfully bites my upper lip. Chill bumps rise up along the back of my arms and neck. I can feel his erection building and pressing against me. It is undeniable, he wants this too.

"You can," he laughs and grazes my ear with his mouth.

"And did," I laugh.

He pulls me close again, parting my mouth with his gentle tongue, coaxing. We kiss for a long time, enamored of each other's smooth, soft, warmth. He traces the edges of my bra with his index finger, following the contours of the lace all the way across my ribcage and across my back to the clasp. I am tremulous and yearning, but just as I anticipate that he is about to undo the clasp, he pauses abruptly and grasps my hand.

"Can I show you something?" There it is, his charming and captivating smile once again, this time in the moonlight.

Chapter Nineteen

My hand in his, Ben leads me through the gardens and down to the edge of the lake. There are rowboats tied up along a dock. We step out onto the rickety wooden boards. There it is, the moon is radiant and lights up the lake like dim sunshine. The half-shaded light somehow helps settle my heart.

"Ginny," he whispers, his eyes are dancing in the reflected light. There is something important he wants to say to me, "You are a startlingly beautiful woman," he adds softly. He says it with such gravity and thirst that for once I feel it to be true.

He steps into a boat and reaches up to touch my face. He traces his thumb along the edge of my lower lip. "Ginny," he exhales slowly, uttering my name like a prayer. He runs his thumb from my lip down my neck and across my shoulder and arm to my hand. Sensations and emotions are rippling through my skin. He grasps my hand between his forefinger and thumb, and I feel a gentle pulling deep within my belly. He kisses first the tips of my fingers and then the contours of my hand, drawing me into the small boat. I feel faint from the motion of the boat and from the unexpected and loving nature of his touch. From such emotional discord to such harmony in one night. It is a sweet warmth through my being; I have never felt like this before.

He sits down in front of me on the bench of the rowboat. He is watching the night sky. I look up at him through my lashes. His face is so beautiful. I hesitate, but I so want to touch him. His jaw is slightly clenched and unshaven. I want to touch my cheek to his cheek. My heart is racing as he untethers the boat from its mooring.

"What are you doing?" I ask.

"Buckle up," he settles back into his seat and smiles. "I want to take you to the middle of the lake."

"But this isn't our boat?"

"I know." Ben assures me, "That's part of the fun of it."

I turn to grab the dock. He smiles at me, "Look up."

The night sky is profoundly dark now and filled with stars. The white tips of the mountains are enflamed by the light of the moon. The air is warm and still. He slowly dips the oars into the delicate water and we drift out into the darkness. I can hear my heart pounding in my ears as my adrenaline surges.

I am wearing Jacqui's pink dress. She tucked it in my suitcase before I left with a note attached, "For a special occasion," it had read. The dress cuts low and hugs against my hips, the bottom edge pools in the bottom of the boat and makes me feel even more exposed. I can feel the water soaking in the hem of the dress. I gather the hem in my hand and tuck it behind my knees. Ben looks at me with an intensity that sets my belly on fire.

I keep telling myself that everything is going to be fine over and over again. My breath is shaky and I try to sync it into the rhythm of the paddling. Ben's gaze is locked on me. He is studying me the way an artist studies a canvas. There is a vividness to the moment that is purely rousing. He is watching me and I am watching him and we are paddling deeper and deeper into the lake. I am not accustomed to this type of attention. I am fighting my impulse to hide, knowing full well that there is nowhere to go, and that ultimately, that's a very good thing.

"I think we've arrived," he whispers softly and tucks the paddles safely in the bottom of the boat. He looks around and decides to pull a handful of life jackets from the bench seat behind him and arranges them delicately on the floor of the boat. I am afraid to look him in the eye because every time I look at him I have a physiological reaction, his eyes, my belly. His gaze is soft and loving. He leans forward, and suddenly I can feel the warmth of his breath against my skin. I feel my body respond. I have never wanted a man like this.

As he moves towards me, the boat lurches side to side, I grasp instinctively for his hand.

"Don't worry, I've got you," he says with a gravelly depth to his voice. He does. I'm his. He pauses, "And I'm not letting go."

My whole body responds to his words. That's what I want. *I want him to never let me go.* My face flushes and a warming ardor melts all the way down my body. My hand is now shaking with the low fever of desire and longing. The sensations are taking over, like something I have never felt.

"Come here," he pulls me towards him. "You're shaking," he takes off his jacket and drapes it over my shoulders to keep me warm.

"That's not why I am shaking," I murmur and smile.

His whole face lights up, "Would you like some more wine?"

"Sure." Why not? I am already in the middle of Lake Geneva on a stolen boat with a man I hardly know whom I'm growing more crazy for by the minute. Maybe it can help quell my deep anxiety.

"Yes, please," I whisper.

"Here." He hands me the bottle of wine.

I scoot forward and lean backwards into the piles of life vests for a better view of the stars. The city is glimmering in the distance.

"This is so good, better than I even imagined," Ben says as he takes and sips the wine, but my mind and body both simultaneously know that he is not talking about the wine.

It's not at all what I expected him to say. So he has been imagining this? Do I have so much to learn? He looks over at me and we watch each other, staring into one another's eyes for an unknown and awesome amount of time, the air between us beckoning. It's a pull that's stronger than the wind. I can barely breath. His eyes are enlivened, taking it all in. My whole body is trembling with desire. It's as involuntary as a fire. All of the books said it, but I have never felt it before, and now here I am fully lit. I am totally ablaze for this man.

He reaches out and touches my lip again. The water around us is still, perfectly reflecting the stars in the sky above us. The sounds of the city are distant. Neither of us can utter a word. The gravitation between us intoxicating. I reach for his cheek and graze my thumb along his stubble. The tug and pull of my thumb along his jawline is almost unbearable. He reaches for my tousled braid and trails it forward along my collarbone. He undoes the hair tie and unfurls the loose strands, slowly combing his fingers through my hair. I look down because the profound tenderness is overwhelming. I lay all the way back pulling him towards me as I fall backwards. My other hand reaches for his blonde curls that I have yearned to touch. I pull his mouth to mine. Our tongues intertwine again and again, this time with a pulse. I feel a low and deep groan reverberate through his throat. The heat between us is prolonged and building, and I feel his full weight release down onto me.

"Are you okay? Are you comfortable?" he asks earnestly as he breathes into the kiss.

He breaks free for a moment and looks into my eyes with a depth that stirs the deepest part of me.

I nod and start to giggle. He catches my mouth again and again mid-giggle. His kiss is light and takes my breath away. Delicate and playful kisses turn to longer melting ones, his tongue, my tongue. There is no doubt that I have never been kissed like this before, not even close.

He reaches down along my breast, past my thigh and his hand gathers my skirt. He lifts it exposing my thigh, kneading, tenderly, exploring. No one has ever touched me like this either. The warmth between us makes all the hairs stand alive. He gently pulls my panties down my legs, placing them carefully beside us. I lick his jawline through to his ear. I notice the dimple in his cheek and am taken by its charm. He pulls his shirt over his head.

In the moonlight I see his beautiful pale skin, barely making out the delicate freckles. His shoulders are notably broader, his arms more muscular, his waist more tapered than I expected. I have never considered myself someone with a particular type or demand in terms of body type, but for a moment I am truly taken aback by the beauty of his physique. I lick the vein that rises up his arm. He rolls me on top of him, pulling my dress over my head. I look around. We are alone, the water rhythmically lapping the edges of the boat. He pulls his pants off and lets them fall away. We are both naked. We lace our fingers together. I trace my tongue from his sternum to his navel. I pause, looking into his eyes, they are burning for me. Completely taking me in. This is desire. I pull him into my mouth. He is hot and throbbing. I lick and taste him. I want to know this part of him, as intimately as I can. My tongue swirls. He grazes the soft inside of my cheek and he groans deeply. "Soft places to soft places" Jacqui always told me. I want to hear and learn all of his pleasure noises. I look at him. He pulls me up to his mouth. I open my thighs to him. He is tracing circles on my back with his finger. He draws his finger slowly across my hip to my labia and draws the same almost torturously teasing circles. Pleasure reverberates up and down my spine.

Like drops of warm water, he places kisses all the way down my neck and belly. Kisses all the way down. Then he leans down and licks all of my soft places, slowly and sensually until I can offer no more tension or resistance. I am melting, simply dissolving into his arms.

"You are so beautiful," at last he sinks slowly, deeply inside me.

We are naked beneath the stars. Fully exposed. The heat and pull and throb and ache. He traces my nipples with his tongue. He squeezes my thighs. Could this burn me down? He is fully inside of me, and but for the rocking of the boat, barely moving. We are making love, slowly, igniting ourselves on fire.

I frame his face with my hands and kiss him deeply. My hand runs through his hair, his soft curls. He is the slowest, sweetest lover. I feel like I am evaporating into the heat of our bodies. My mind turns off, and I gaze into his eyes as he laces our fingers once again.

"Ginny," he cries and something in the way he looks at me and says my name tips me over into ecstasy. "Ginny," he moans as he pulses and ripples inside of me. He bites my thumb and we come together. My whole body tenses and then everything melts away.

Chapter Twenty

I lay my head down along Ben's chest and listen to his heart racing, this heart that is now instantly so important to me. I can feel the thin film of his sweat along my cheek. I have never, ever felt this closely held by another person; my whole body releases into him. The stars blink above us.

He is looping my hair in his fingers, "You know what I have noticed?"

"What's that?"

"That you have no idea how beautiful you are."

"What?" I have also never been in a conversation like this.

"You don't. You have no idea what a pleasure it is to look at you, to just lay here like this and look at you in the moonlight."

He traces his finger along my belly to my hip.

I stare at him blankly, a deer in the head lights.

"See, you don't even know how to respond to what I am saying," he laughs and kisses me.

"It's true, I don't."

"I feel like you've lived in denial of this basic fact about you and the world, and some people took advantage of your lack of..." he paused and searched for the word.

"Self-awareness. That's not even the right way to say it. You lack nothing at all. That is really the whole thing of it; you are the complete package, the brains, the beauty, but most importantly the heart."

He grasps my hand and touches my heart with both his hand and mine entwined; a warmth trickles through me, from my toes all the way to my forehead and then once again the tears start to flow. As they drop off one by one, he kisses them away. Like this, we drift off to sleep.

***

It's not the thunder but the raindrops that wake me, landing first upon my cheek and then down the contours of my naked body. I reach around in the dark and reach for my dress, fumbling as I pull it over my head as though its fabric will somehow protect me from the rain.

Ben is still naked and laughing as he watches me scrambling in the boat. I pause a minute, and looking back down at him, I tilt my head to his, kissing him deeply first up along his neck, then finding his mouth, drops of rain falling from the curls of his hair along my cheek, washing the last remnants of my tears away. It feels so incredibly good to move with someone in this way. The boat is unsteady from the wind and the rain. It is all very disorienting, yet fun. I can feel Ben smiling through our kiss. His hands gently running up and down the curves of my waist, softly grasping my hips. A flash of lightening is loud and close, and it scares me. Ben pulls me into his lap and sets the oars. I am having trouble pulling my lips away from his as we make our way back to the distant blurry lights of the rain soaked city. The raindrops are cold but I can barely feel them against my skin. Ben is lit up and gorgeous in the flashing lights of the storm. It is like something out of a Turner painting.

When we return to the dock, I am drenched and shivering.

"You're freezing," he observes. "Do you want to go back home?"

"No, that is not my home." I shudder at the thought of Fredrick's melancholy apartment and, even more so, at the thought of leaving Ben's side.

"Then do you want to come back to my apartment? You can take a shower. We can dry your clothes."

I nod readily, "I do."

Chapter Twenty-One

Ben lives on the top floor of his building, his hand guides me as we wind our way up the staircase. We stop at each floor to kiss; we can do nothing else. We kiss in the doorway. It's ridiculously romantic; like bees drawn to pollen, his kiss is my nectar.

As we move inside his apartment, I am struck by the light that penetrates the darkness. The walls in the living room are mostly windows; the lights of the city are blinking and everywhere, the lightning still flashing.

"You are cold to the bone, let me run you a bath."

He disappears for a moment and comes back with a robe and a towel. He lifts my dress off me and shakes his head, most approvingly, looking me up and down.

"You are *so* sexy."

He wraps me in a plush periwinkle blue terry cloth bathrobe and pulls off his own shirt as he leads me down the hallway to the bath. I am shivering. *He* is so sexy! His body is truly gorgeous. I cannot help but smile at his beautiful chest, his broad shoulders, his toned abdomen. I could go on, but decide it's not polite to stare.

"Do you want me to make some tea? I don't want you to catch a cold," he says as he gestures to the run bath.

"No thank you, but I'd like you to get in with me," I say, shyly looking up at him.

It still all feels so unreal, but I am going with it. This handsome and sweet man standing there looking at me. It seems out of a fantasy.

"Are you sure?"

I step forward and grasp the waistband of his pants, fumbling to unbutton them.

"Yes. I'm very, very sure."

I let the robe fall to the floor and kiss him deeply as I step backwards into the bath blindly, hoping that I don't stumble or fall in my attempt, but also knowing somehow that he will catch me if I do. The water feels hot to my chilled body and he watches me with concentration as I settle into the bath. I look up and grasp his hand, leading him into the tub. He leans his back into me. I let my fingers drift along the smooth contours of his body. I am soaking it all in. This bath. This moment in time. His skin. All of the concerns of the day have left me, and I am here now. As if reading my thoughts, he turns and says,

"Ginny, can you stay with me?" His words are candid, spoken aloud to me as he thinks them himself. "The thought of you back in his lair," his mouth and the corners of his eyes become tense, "I don't even really have the words. It's just that I watched as he took you for granted. He couldn't even see you."

Ben touches the back of his neck.

"He had told me that his work consumed him; that he hadn't had time or patience for…. But I thought with me, things would change—love would change it, shift his sedimented habits. I was naive. It doesn't really work like that. Not for long. Not that I know that much about love, or even….."

"You haven't had a lot of experiences in that arena?"

"Correct, and it was more like a mechanical power play. Animalistic without the tenderness. It was nothing like I thought it would be." I start to cry again. "What was I thinking?" I look up at him.

Nothing is as I thought it would be. Fredrick is not the man I deluded myself into believing he was. And now here I am naked in a bathtub with Ben, gorgeous and naked, but that's not even what makes him so sexy. Really, it is his tenderness that draws me in. His soft, supple skin that matches his soft nature, the gentleness of his touch and the equally gentle way he listens to me with his eyes.

Ben looks deeply at me, tucking my hair behind my ear. He is taking it all in.

"Look Ginny, none of this matters right now. You are safe and wanted here. I want you to stay, I want you so much..." he hesitates again and closes his eyes, "Please stay."

I nod and wrap my arms around his neck. He frames my face with his hands. He kisses my cheeks, the tears from my eyes, my forehead, my smile lines, my chin, my nose. He is peppering me with kisses. Soon the kisses include gentle licks with his tongue and he is exploring my face. My eyelids, my ears, the underside of my chin, my neck. He traces circles around my nipples, first with his finger so gently, and then bends down and with his tongue takes me in his mouth. My nipples respond, longingly. My mind goes blank with sensation. Instinctively, I pull his finger into my mouth and begin to swirl my tongue around and around. I pull him into the water and wrap my legs around his torso. I guide him gently into me. We are moving in the water's warm embrace; it's holding us both. His hands kneading my buttocks, my head thrown back. I wrap my arms around his neck and retrace the journey his tongue made along my own body. Pleasure begets pleasure and I feel the tingling heat climb up my spine. I close my eyes and unravel into his arms, the orgasm spiraling up and down my spine again and again. First me, then him. He waited so he could watch me.

"So beautiful," is all he says as he kisses my face, his strong hand on my hair. He presses his forehead to mine.

***

I am exhausted. He dries me off with a towel and hangs my dress by the window, leading me down the hallway to his bedroom. He pulls back the covers and watches me as I climb in. He follows me, wraps his arms around me, and kisses me lovingly, and we drift off to sleep, holding each other.

Chapter Twenty-Two

The morning sun peeks through the cream curtains. The bed is warm from our sleep. As I feel my body awaken, I feel something else. Ben's hand reaches over and very gently strokes me, as if to make sure I am still here, to reassure himself that I am, that we are not a dream. He is half asleep, barely awake, but hard, to say the least. Very sleepily, he rolls on top of me. His eyes are half closed, as if to remain half in dreamland, yet half in waking life. This is our liminal space. It is still quite dark in the room, but in the gentle light that seeps in from the slit in the curtain, his sexy, somnolent smile is apparent. We are both completely naked, his arms by my shoulders. He so easily holds himself up, just hovering above me, effortlessly, almost floating, soaring. Those arms. I run my hand along his triceps. I had no idea an upper arm could elicit such longing and desire.

Ben kisses my lips so gently, and without a sound, without any words, not so much as a 'good morning,' I feel him enter me, unceremoniously, without a hint of doubt, as if this is just how he wakes up in the morning, how we will, how we are. It's as if his body knows just where to go and requires no guidance or assistance. He finds his home inside me and he effortlessly slips in. I moan, welcoming his arrival, as if the night next to each other but still separate was too long. He feels so exquisite inside me, fitting perfectly. He rhythmically thrusts into me, hovering above me. The rest of the world is still; there is only the movement of his slow, strong, yet tender thrust. We are silent, not speaking. It's all I can feel, physically and emotionally. It's my whole world. He groans in pleasure. I run my hands along his back, his muscular, strong back. It is simple. It is good. So good. I moan with pleasure as I feel his length go in and out of me, as if massaging my insides, a morning massage from the inside out, until we both come from the pure and simple gratification of movement. Somehow this is all we need. And I think to myself, "Now this is the way to wake up in the morning."

As we lay in a quiet embrace, he speaks, "Ever since I saw you in the cathedral, I've dreamed of you at night, dreamed of making love with you. And when I leave my dreams, I instinctively roll over hoping to find you, only to have a rude awakening when you're not there. But this morning, you are right where you are supposed to be." He kisses me.

I can only respond with a smile of complete delight. I am speechless. He smiles at my smile and languidly moves out of bed to start the morning. I am left resting with a sense of immense unreality mixed with real pleasure. Could this be my life?

***

As I'm lying in bed, he sits in a chair beside me, his legs and feet propped on the bed, and he watches me drink my morning coffee with relish. I notice just how very beautiful his feet are. The perfect arch, compact, strong yet incredibly attractive—and surprisingly well groomed toes. Oh boy, I'm a goner.

Ben smiles at me and speaks, "I love how you enjoy that."

"The sex or the coffee?"

"Both."

"Well they're both sooooo darn good. Who knew? I am so thankful for coffee. And....for you, for this."

He smiles at me, just watching me drink it up. His gaze seems completely taken by my presence. I feel more seen and happier than I have in a very long time.

"So, let's see. What else is on the agenda today, besides love making? How about galleries? Do you have a preference for one?"

I blush to think that I really do not. "You know, I'm afraid to say I don't, and actually, in truth, I feel pretty ignorant when it comes to art."

"Well, tell me, which paintings you've enjoyed so far? What are your favorites?"

I start to feel embarrassed; "There aren't many. I can't even really say. To be honest, I'm worried that my lackluster appreciation for art may be a reflection of my own dullness. I mean, being with you, I can already tell art has greatly influenced your life, and I envy that. It can shape a person; I get that. But in general, while I've studied the usual art history greats, I've tended of late to put art aside as if it's a luxury. My focus has been on work, solving the problems of the world...." I make sure to say it with an ironic laugh, since it sounds pretentious and defensive even to me, but I actually mean it. I also leave out that I've been a tad too melancholy to appreciate the beauty of Geneva, and to even see outside of myself. To view art one looks outward, in order to return inward I imagine, but lately, there has been too little outward gazing.

Ben kindly responds, "Well maybe we can do both—help the world and enjoy the art. And since we are in Geneva, I say we go for it. We can enjoy the city together. Heck, let's enjoy each other through the city and its art. That sounds good to me; I like this plan, and I'm pretty sure it will better the world. It will better my world, I guarantee."

"Sounds like an excellent plan to me, sign me up," and my smile feels like it permeates my whole body. I feel like one giant smile.

"And for the record, Ginny, I think that *you* see things that others don't. And nothing, and I mean nothing, about you is lackluster. Just the opposite. Geneva has never been so bright as with you in it. Trust me."

My heart swells and veritably moves towards him. This must be what is meant by pulling at one's heartstrings. He is my magnetic pull. Heart to heart. I am struck that even though he is an aesthete, not only does he not belittle me for a lack of artistic appreciation or condescend to me (as if I unconsciously expect it, having gotten sadly accustomed to such a reaction from the time I've spent with Fredrick), but instead Ben cheerfully takes my confession as an opportunity for us to grow closer and to make me feel better about myself. Oh how good it feels to be in loving company. It's like a window in a prison cell. These are clichés, I know, but it really is like breathing fresh spring air and feeling the warmth of sunshine after being shut-in all dreary, cold winter. Clichés are clichés for a reason, and I feel like I'm finally figuring out, on a sensational level, what they actually mean. It's almost as if I've been parroting language for a long time, and now the meanings of the words are actually sinking in and coming to life, just as I am.

I continue on this topic, knowing that as glorious as his kiss is, it is also important to speak.

"It's quite a unique combination, you know, to be so interested and engaged in both art and political theory. Is there a career for that? Could you make something of that particular combination?"

Ben smiles, "Politics and art are both very important to me—but honestly I haven't spent much time thinking about how to commodify them like that. That's not really my thing. I like them for their own sakes, not particularly as a means to prestige or fortune."

There is something very romantic about Ben. But at the same time, I hear my father's practical, protective voice and I have to ask, "But isn't making a living important to you?"

"Let's just say, it hasn't been a driving force in my life."

I take a deep breath, "Then what is?"

"Right now? Spending time with you. I can think of no better fortune." He laughs. "I know that sounds over the top, but it's true."

He touches his thumb to my chin and there it is again, that pull, like one magnet to another, he leans in and we are drawn together, mouth to mouth, tongue to tongue. I gently step over his lap and straddle him. I wrap myself fully around him. He envelops me. Forehead to forehead, we rest. I can feel the heat of his pulse.

Chapter Twenty-Three

"But one cannot live on love alone," I think to myself as my father's voice breaks through the marching rhythm of Ben's pulse. I am more pragmatic than romantic, and Ben's response worries me a little. But I am not at all ready or in the mood to tackle the topic of financial security, so I continue the conversation about art. Ben's mind is fascinating to me. I enjoy the way he sees things, including and most of all, at the moment, me.

I respond, "As I articulate it out loud to you, it's like my aversion to art may be somewhat symptomatic. I suppose my intentions and energy have been mainly directed towards service and work. I don't remember making that choice, consciously, but sitting here with you, that's what is coming into relief. Ben, why does it seem like life comes more easily for you? You seem to go with what comes naturally. I feel like I've been forcing it, almost like I've embraced drudgery without even realizing it. Sometimes I think I was attracted to Fredrick for his mind alone, and even more for his resounding work ethic—it made mine seem normal if not tame. The man works all the time. In comparison, I was starting to think of myself as lazy. And I'm pretty sure by most standards, I'm really not."

Ben looks slightly annoyed, "Well, don't compare yourself negatively, I certainly don't see such ways helping Fredrick in the least. His obsession with the minutiae ultimately blinds him to the big picture. His work is so detailed, but it fundamentally adds up to nothing. He thinks the work will just take care of itself. But that's not the case. And that tendency certainly blinded him to you. Which, I'd say, proves my point, in the biggest way. *Not* smart."

At first I'm taken aback by such a comment about Fredrick's shortcomings. Ben's points cut to the heart of who Fredrick is. Fredrick's work ethic did garner my admiration. There is a part of me that still needs someone, Ben, anyone, to say that Fredrick *is* wise and worthy of the accolades he has received, because if I don't have that—if he does *not* have those qualities—then what is there and what *was* I thinking? Am I offended on Fredrick's behalf or my own, at his stupidity or mine, or both? It's looking like both, but ultimately, I'd only have mine to blame.

I am quiet for a moment, finding myself looking at the ground. I see Ben looks a bit bashful. Does he pick up on my offense? He is very sensitive to my emotions. That in itself takes me aback. His keen and loving receptiveness is so very different from what I've experienced lately.

"I mean obviously Fredrick works very diligently."

I can tell that Ben is back-peddling to make me feel better. Though his comment is somewhat hollow and falls flat, I still appreciate his attempt, his good-naturedness and good humor. He palpably cares about my feelings.

He continues, "I'm sorry if I offended you. I should really keep such thoughts to myself. It's just that I want you to be happy. That's what I care about."

Normally, my anxiety would take over, but this time I let it subside, I let myself wonder more openly. I wonder how I would ultimately take an attitude like Ben's, one so different from my own. Ben's go with the flow approach is actually more like Jacqui's style. I haven't encountered many academics of this ilk. But perhaps instead of finding it grating, I would find it refreshing; perhaps it would even be a beneficial influence on me?

How different life could be if I chose to be with such a partner. On the one hand, if I chose a man more like Fredrick, I'd have a life of steady work, from library to potentially the UN floor, on the other hand, with a man like Ben, we'd be deciding at the spur of the moment that today is going to be more like a vacation. Oh to take a mini-vacation on a Friday afternoon with my love, heck on a Wednesday! Life would have such a different tenor. And here he is, Ben, showing me what this life could look like, in actual time.

What a difference a partner can make. It can affect one's whole life, each day, each hour, in such a profound way. Given that, it seems like one should give this, one's choice of a partner, a great deal of thought. What's more significant? Ah, one's "significant other," that's why it's so named; I'm starting to get it. These phrases are finding their meanings for me—they are finally landing.

Where I once thought there was nothing more important than good work and a partner who strove for the same, I'm beginning to see there is much more at stake—one's mood, for example, one's way of moving through life, one's everyday activities, one's moment by moment. Does everyone know this? Am I so late to the game? Well at least I'm in the game now.

But for some reason, instead of dwelling on the essential, I stupidly blurt out, "Fredrick does not approve of such laissez-faire attitudes towards work and life."

Ben is silent a moment, looks me intently in the eyes (those fire-blue eyes!) and slowly, quietly replies, "Yes. I realize Fredrick and I are very different. And I don't know if it's possible for a woman who loves him to then love me."

His words hang heavy in the air between us.

Now I am the back-peddler, "Wait. No. I mean to say I am so glad you are different, and that you are as you are. I'm just trying to understand..." I let my words trail off.

I feel myself blush; Ben takes my face in-between his hands, at once delicate and yet impossibly strong. He brings his face closer to mine and gently, so very softly that I think I might melt into a pool on the floor, kisses my lips. Such soft lips, such a beautiful embrace. He cups my face. I am at once perfectly content. My whole body softens, as if the armored way I hold every muscle just relaxes in his arms. His eyes, his hands, his kisses, are all magical to me. I don't need to be anywhere else when we embrace like this; I only want to rest here.

He pushes me gently and playfully back onto the bed. "I'm not finished with you yet," he says and kisses my lips, my neck, my right breast and then my left, as if not to make one jealous of the other. His lips and tongue circle my nipples slowly and scrumptiously, my nipples rise to him, practically begging his mouth to take them, and he takes all the time he and I need, before he makes his way down, kissing me all over until he arrives at my inner thigh. He gently places a kiss on my right thigh and then my left and then makes his way to my yearning middle. His tongue is somehow both strong and gentle at the same time, as he licks and sucks me. He presses down with his hand on my skin, just below my abdomen, somewhere I can't quite describe, and the pressure of his hand combined with the tease of his tongue elicits a feeling I have never felt before. He places his strong fingers inside me. He alternates between deep pressure from his one hand, tickling with his mouth and tongue, and filling me up with his other hand. Then all happen simultaneously. I look down to see the light that rises from his smiling eyes as he looks up at me. My back arches and he holds my hips. I moan and groan and writhe in his arms giving myself over to him entirely. I'm his. He owns me. I am panting breathlessly in his arms. I release and in so doing let out a deep cry. I grab him and bring him up to me. I kiss his mouth and he lays on top of me. Curbing the sweet shivers and quakes of my coming with the weight of his body. It's as if my body is pronouncing my heart quakes, a woman could get used to this.

Chapter Twenty-Four

As the intensity of the pleasure gently subsides, I think about Ben's last comment before he went down on me so exquisitely. I was aware that Ben had many questions as to why I had chosen to be with Fredrick. I suspected that Ben most likely thought it to be a character flaw in myself (which it may very well be), but I think now Ben's mind is changing. I decide not to take his comment as a condemnation of choices, but as a genuine desire to get to know me and understand me more, and maybe even ultimately to be with me. My heart leaps at the thought. Me. And wait, did he say he was questioning how *I might love him?* Did he say *love?*

It's as if Ben knows what I'm thinking about. He takes my hand, "Ginny, as I get to know you, I realize more and more that you are not anything like him. I know you think you are, but you aren't. You are far more clever than he is. You don't think that, but *you are*. In so many ways, and you're not cold like he is. Just the opposite. You are sunshine. I think you mistook Fredrick's studiousness for valor and weaved a romance in your head out of a fantasy, in part because you see the goodness of hard work and the goodness in people, even when and where others don't. You are the warmest, most open person I have ever met. You are full of feelings, even if you don't want to be. I think you are amazing.

I am incredibly thankful to be in your company. And when I hold you like this, I feel like I'm holding everything that matters."

As I take in Ben's words, I realize he sees me in the most appreciative light. With Ben it's a different kind of companionship. I can be myself. With Fredrick I feel I am always attempting to be what he wants, yet, at the same time, always falling short. And falling short was inevitable. When faced with impossible demands, one can never fulfill desire.

Once again, Ben could condemn my decisions but he sees the misguided but loving place from which they came. In addition to the amazingly intimate sex, I have never before felt so lovingly regarded. Perhaps the two go hand in hand?

Ben unfortunately went on, "Of course it does suck that Fredrick is technically my boss. Without him I have no graduate research stipend and would not be able to finish my dissertation, not without taking a lot longer—having to find and perform a job and find another supervisor. And I'm guessing he's none too pleased with me, right about now, given these particular givens. Or certainly, won't be when he figures it all out, if he hasn't already."

He pauses with an earnestness that makes me even more attentive,

"But you know what Ginny, honestly, the more I care about you, the less I care about any of that."

I am deeply struck by his last sentiment. I sit in a smiling silence and let his words marinate.

But for the first time, coming out of the hazy, luscious daze of great sex, it dawns on me that by allowing myself, us, to engage in such activities, I have put Ben in a dangerous and precarious place career wise and wonder how I, of all people, could have been so careless. Our bodies recognize for the first time that there is gravity beneath our feet. I decide to check my phone at long last.

Five missed calls from Fredrick, no message, and three missed calls from Jacqui.

***

There are nasty complications to be sure, and they are all too real, but the entire day stands before us and we decide to live it fully and in the way we most wish. We are dressed (at last), and fed, somewhat, although my stomach was so filled with excitement that I could hardly choke more than a few bites down. I am distracted sitting next to Ben. And as much as I love food, and as delicious as the chocolate croissants he retrieved from the bakery next door are, my bodily attention is very much focused on and filled up by Ben's presence. When he asks me what I like most to do on a beautiful day, I tell him go for a walk and talk, and he replies without skipping a beat, "Then that's what we'll do."

The idea of spending the day walking through this beautiful, old European city with Ben sounds like heaven, but I have a nagging feeling and need to voice it, "But I'm concerned that I will spend a large part of our walk worrying that Fredrick will be looking for me. He's called several times already."

We exchange a knowing glance because in our hearts, while this seems a reasonable woe, we both suspect that he will not. We both imagine that Fredrick will be glued to his library desk scanning my thesis for any cracks or leaks for which he can berate me. I fear that he is slowly shaving my dissertation down into a pointed weapon against me.

"I have an idea then," Ben tenderly grabs my face and looks me deeply in the eyes. "We will spend the day at Mont Saleve. There is no chance that Fredrick would ever go there. Rest and wait here for just a bit," he kisses my cheeks again and again. "I will make some arrangements and then we will leave."

He dashes out the door and I fall back into his bed. The sheets
are soft and baby blue. They are saturated with the smell of Ben in
the morning. I wrap myself in the comforter and find a deep and
warm comfort—ah a 'comforter.' I get it now. I reach over and
grab my purse. I grab my phone. Another missed call. It is Jacqui
and she has once again not left a message. I am in no mood to talk
right now, but she is my dear sister, so I text her.

"U ok?"

She responds immediately, "Yes... but what about you?"

"Never better," I respond, "will explain later," and put my
phone away.

***

Ben's apartment is the opposite of Fredrick's. It is sparse and
soft. Light filters in from every direction. It is small but very
homey.

The bed is big and close to the ground. I notice that even
though the bedroom is small, it feels bright and roomy. There is
not much in it. A plant, his bed, some candles, incense. In turn, it
feels like there is so much room for us here, physically and
emotionally. Besides a few rather strategically placed mirrors,
there are not a lot of things to distract our minds or hearts. It
occurs to me that one can be very much in the moment in this
room, without things or objects pulling you in one direction or the
other, neither pulling one's thoughts into the past nor pushing one
into the future. I wonder if this is intentional. It seems wise. I
think for a moment, that I may have a lot to learn from Ben. I
laugh...to think that I have possibly found a teacher in this
particular form....a teacher in such a gorgeous package as Ben.

I get up and walk into the living room. An inviting grey rug
with a swirled cream design calls to me. It is so soft under my feet.
We will make love on this rug. I flush at the thought. There are

many charcoal drawings lining the walls. They are mostly cityscapes and I have a feeling they are from Ben's own hand.

I wander over to his bookshelf. The top shelf is filled with the likes of Checkov, Dickens, Greene, Munro, and Delillo. The man obviously loves to read great literature. The lower shelf holds books on Nelson Mandela, The Dalai Llama, Joseph Campbell, some books on meditation, and then four or five more books on tantra. I had suspected that Ben has a deep spiritual side from some of the things he had said to me. And while I am familiar with some of the books' topics, I have never been bold enough to ever pick up a book on tantra. I reach for the first book I see, *Tantric Love*. It sounds fairly basic. I curl up on the floor and start to flip to the table of contents.

Love and Spirit, Mastering Love, Orgasm as a Spiritual Experience, The Source of Orgasmic States, Relaxing into Orgasm.

I drop the book like a hot potato as Ben bursts through the door with contagious excitement. He is carrying one of my totes from Fredrick's apartment. He looks down at my flushed face and at the book I've discarded on the floor and smiles.

"Been doing a little light reading while I've been gone, I see," he teases.

I flush an even deeper shade of red. I want to crawl underneath the grey rug.

He grabs the book from the floor and tucks it under his arm.

"This is a good book to start with," his whole face is glimmering with excitement.

I follow him into the bedroom, as he dumps the contents of my bag onto the bed. There are my jeans, a tank top, various clothing articles, my running shoes, some socks and underwear.

"I just couldn't choose," he smiles and lifts some underwear off the bed with his finger.

My face reddens. I didn't know that it could be this way, so fun and so playful.

"How did you do that?"

"Thankfully the 'errand boy' usually has a key to the master's door. And more importantly, we have just an hour until the bus leaves for Mont Saleve."

He fishes through the pile of underwear until he finds what he is looking for and hands them to me, "Please, for me." he smiles again.

I am still wearing his t-shirt and scramble clumsily to the bathroom to change. He has chosen the one pair Jacqui sent with me—they are of course, the sexiest underwear I own, by far. I haven't even worn them. For outerwear, I decide upon a loose fitting romper. It is sleeveless and navy blue and airy. I like the way it feels against my skin and it smells like Jacqui, just the infusion of confidence I need. I look in the mirror for the first time. My hair is a mess. I pull it to the front and loosely braid it. I take a deep breath and step out from the bathroom.

He is there again, touching himself and waiting for me to emerge. His smile engulfs me as I stand there awkwardly. He reaches his hand to me, pulling my lacy bra strap free. He slides his finger up and then down the satin. And we begin again, the pull that I have no power to fight. My body craves this man. I crave his mouth, his hands, my fingers in his hair—every inch of him. I have never been held like this before.

Chapter Twenty-Five

"Where are we headed?"

"Ah, no worries my companera .. carpe diem." Ben smiles and squeezes my hand.

I'm aware that he is mixing his languages, but I don't care. I like it. With his hand in mine, I can visibly relax. He is right, seize the day; his attitude and candor are such a contrast and a relief to everything that has happened since I arrived in Geneva.

He looks me up and down and shakes his head, "You are just so stunning. I could look at you all day. How is it possible you could stay so hidden?"

I look down at my hands, "I'm not really sure." I hesitate and look over at Ben. His eyes are shining and have the look of a glacial lake, greens and blues swirled together in the center, the light reflecting off of the golden middle. His lips and cheeks are tinted rose by the blush of the sun.

I continue, "I guess I just spent a lot of my time taking care of my mom, and when she died, I started to take care of my father and sister. That seemed most important. I just had no desire to go out with my peers, or to parties, really no desire to date. I just wanted to stay home and read."

"Was there someone important before Fredrick?"

"Not really. Nothing serious. It's ok. Jacqui has dated enough for both of us." I laugh to myself. "There were guys who were interested, but I just asked them to be my friend. It felt safer that way. What about you?"

"I've dated a number of women, one woman I almost married."

"What happened?"

"It just didn't work out. I was young, I was choosing unconsciously, based more on past relations that weren't the best protocols. It took a little too long for me to figure it out than it should have, but thank goodness I did. For many reasons, but mainly, so I can be here, with you."

He looks over at me again. I love his smile. I can feel the day getting warmer and brighter. The noise of the city is retreating.

I grasp his hand, "So really, where are we heading?"

"Trust me, you'll love it." He pulls me into his arms.

***

As we start up Mont Saleve, Ben bounces from rock to rock. We are hiking. The trail is steep and winding.

"Are you up for this?"

"Carpe Diem! I'm up for anything," I sing out. I'm feeling a bit like Maria in the Sound of Music.

The trail is so steep that when I turn around, I feel like I'm flying.

Ben's lips catch my mouth as I turn back to face the steep slope of the mountain. He kisses me deeply, without hesitation. He is always so near to me. It makes me feel so much less lonely than I have of late. We can see the cable car approaching behind us. The view of Lake Geneva and the city itself is spectacular, even from the first parts of the climb. He holds out his hand to me as I clamber over a steep rock. As we climb higher, my excitement mounts.

Mont Saleve is a different world from Geneva. It is the Switzerland of storybooks with views of the mountain, the lake and the Rhone valley. Part way up, we arrive in the small village of Monnetier. It is a quaint town with one main street and a cluster of homes and a chapel. As we walk through the town, Ben holds my hand and leads me into the small chapel. It is beautiful and totally empty. There is an alcove off to the side of the church. We sit down in front of the altar and face each other. He reaches in his backpack and pulls out the book, the very one he caught me reading in his apartment just a few hours earlier. Once again I flush in embarrassment. He smiles and brushes my hair out of my face and opens the book.

He reads aloud, "In Sanskrit, *tantra* can be translated as expansion or transformation. Five thousand years ago, tantra understood that we are a balance of inner opposites and through sexual union a spiritual alchemy can happen that allows us to transmute our energy, liberate our mind and balance and attain our full potential…" He looks away from the book towards me, "Are you still with me?" he asks and squeezes my hand.

I smile and nod.

He looks pleased and continues to read, "Passion is about presence. Ginny, there is so much to this…want to explore it?"

I nod.

"Here cross hands, let's try this," he crosses our hands so that his right hand is holding my left hand and his left is holding my right, crosswise.

"Look into my eyes. When I exhale, you exhale. When I inhale, you inhale. Just notice the breath. It is everything now. Let's breathe as if we are one body, not two. Look into my eyes softly, like this." Our eyes meet. Our gaze is wavering and soft, as inviting as a glimmering pool on a sultry afternoon. Our eyes lock into each other, he smiles airily and we begin to breathe together. His eyes are so full and so beautiful. I am at once scared and fulfilled; time melts and I melt away with it, the breathing in and out, as one, in synchrony....time melds, we meld.

At a certain point, the energy shifts and I feel that familiar pull in my belly. This is it. The desire is taking hold. But this time it is qualitatively different. There is more heat, more knowing. Without thinking or looking away, I move towards him. He squeezes my hand and gathers me to him. He grabs my waist and slowly traces my contours. I place my arms around his shoulders. I smell the back of his neck. I love his smell; I think it is in part the scent of the olive oil soap we used in the bath.

He licks my throat, my ear. He kisses the edges of my eyes. His whole look has changed, the softness of his eyes have given way to desire. This is passion. He holds me closer. I can feel him getting increasingly harder. It's exciting, but we are in a church. I stare into his fire-blues. The pull is almost unbearable. He reaches for the blouse of my romper and unbuttons one after another kissing my neck down to my nape. He reaches in gently touching my nipple. I am sliding up and down and across his erection. We are still fully clothed but the heat between us is almost unbearable. I lean forward and bring his mouth to mine kissing him, our mouths melding together like our breath. My shirt is wide open. He is sliding it over my shoulders, to reveal my breasts to his gaze and touch. He runs his tongue along the outline of my silvery birthmark. Then, like a flash, I break away.

"I can't Ben. I'm sorry. It's too intense, too public," I look away at last.

He is catching his breath. His eyes are cloaked with ardor. Beads of sweat trail along his collarbone. I am fighting my desire to slide my tongue along that groove and taste his salty sweat.

"You take my breath away," he says. "I'm sorry. You're right. I thought we would just meditate here but the energy and chemistry between us just takes hold."

I am beginning to regret that I pulled away. Ben seems lost in his thoughts and hunger for me, for our union. He is coming out of something.

"I'm sorry," I say. "It is just so much, and so public."

"I know," he is buttoning up my shirt sweetly, delicately. "Perhaps later," he says. "When we are alone."

"Yes," I say, "No perhaps. Definitely, please at home." I say not even thinking.

"Home?" he say and smiles. "I like that... at home." He grasps my hand and we head back to the trail.

***

As we reach the top of the mountain, only sky is above us. I can't imagine being anywhere else with anyone else. For one moment, it is perfection in every way. And I feel very lucky.

"Breathtaking," he says "the perfect view." He is looking at me not the landscape.

It is the perfect view. Mont Blanc is in the background. Ben is my foreground, right where I want him.

When we get to the top of the mountain there is a restaurant, L'Horizon. I am starving. It turns out that tantra plus climbing is great for one's appetite. When we are done with our delicious meal, Ben looks at me and says, "Let's go home."

My soul warms at the thought of "our home," and the word 'home' itself has taken on meanings of not just safety and shelter, which it does, but is also now permeated with the significance of love and warmth, comfort and kissing, and love making.

"Yes, please," I say, "Let's go home," and I think to myself, I want to be able to say that phrase, in this way, for a very long time.

Chapter Twenty-Six

"You know, particles collide here, in Geneva." Ben's eyes are beaming with a boyish delight. His arm is tucked beneath his head. "It's a re-creation of the Big Bang…"

He likes to say unexpected things that surprise me, and to watch how I react. He likes to wander amidst the quirky, unexpected places of Geneva, take me to the tiny Ile Rousseau and to look at the jaw-dropping apartment buildings called The Schtroumpfs.

Today, he wants to visit the 17 mile ring of superconducting magnets tucked beneath our feet.

"Are you talking about CERN or is this some new tantric exercise?"

"Can't both be true? After all, both involve exploring the secrets of the universe."

"We can go there, to the physics lab?"

"Yes, we can, observe particles traveling at the speed of light."

"Fascinating," I say and loop my arm through his with delight.

"Nonetheless," he says as he pulls me closer, "we can also rehearse some tantric version too if you would like." His smile is contagious.

"I'll think it over," I say as I tug on the buckle of his belt.

***

We are at one with the science geeks at the edge of the Swiss-French border as we take a service elevator 100m down beneath a sprawl of generic office buildings to the Large Hadron Collider. It is its own underground world of elite physicists and engineers on bikes circling a 17 mile ring of plates, cables, wires, chambers, and tubes. We are here to imagine protons being flung at each other at close to the speed of light. We are in a huge concrete cavern. It's kind of like caving, industrial spelunking that is, and I feel like I am on some space mission. Because Ben is beside me, I have a feeling this will also entail a sexy mission of some sort.

The guide ushers us to the side, "It took over 10 years to design and build it." He is passionate. "It weighs 7,000 tons," he continues. "Welcome to the world's largest scientific experiment."

We all look around the facility in awe.

"But why?" a man asks captiously. "13.25 billion for what?" His arms are folded.

"We built it to help us understand what happened over 13.7 billion years ago. We are trying to re-create the conditions of the very first moments of the universe."

"The Big Bang," Ben whispers in my ear and squeezes my arm. "You know, it doesn't have to be so complicated," he urges, grasping my hand. "A bed, some candles."

I elbow him in the ribs. My whole body is tingling from his breath against my ear and his hand on my lower back. It seems that Ben always has his hands on me, in contact or close proximity with my body, stroking or caressing me. I love it. I particularly adore when his hand is under my hair at the nape of my neck, and he cups the back of my nape gently, massaging softly. Turns out I am much more tactile than I had realized.

The tour guide gestures to the side, "These concrete walls have been erected as radiation shields. There are over 9,300 magnets inside a liquid nitrogen and liquid helium cocktail. That mixture creates a chilly -271 degrees C temperature. We have to make it that cold so that the tens of millions of collisions that happen in a second's time don't destroy the facility," our guide is excited. "We squeeze the protons into beams with a diameter of less than a human hair; one beam one way, then another the other way, and then we make them collide. We break them into pieces in hope of figuring out how the universe works by smashing it apart and looking at the pieces."

"How fast do the protons go?"

"They go around the 17 miles loop 11,000 times a second. We get photos of these miniature Big Bang collisions over and over again. It is teaching us what the universe it made up of." He stares over his shoulder at the collider. "Remember, these are just the patterns though. Ultimately, we are looking for the beautiful and simple math equation that underlies these observations."

"Who works here?" a woman asks from the back of the group.

"Over 10,000 physicists and engineers from 85 countries are collaborating on this project. It's a melding of nations, global harmony in a laboratory. In 2012 we made headlines with the proof of the existence of the Higgs boson. Higgs, it's reckoned, is responsible for our existence. It is what gives mass to particles – that's why it is nicknamed the 'God particle'."

"So 13.25 billion to prove that god exists," the man crosses his arms and laughs to himself.

"That and please know that CERN has already given us the World Wide Web, advances in medical imaging and created particle-beam therapies for cancer. When science and scientists collaborate at this level, there are unexpected discoveries every single day."

"What are the broadest objectives?" I ask.

"The secret of life and the universe," he smiles. "Evidence of black holes, dark matter, we believe that it may make up more than 25% of the galaxy. We are looking for proof of hidden other dimensions."

"Can you talk a little bit about dark matter?" I add in a timid voice, my inner nerd is gleeful.

"From our detailed observations of the universe thus far, we have come to understand that the universe is filled with an unknown substance that we call dark matter. Like many things in physics, we know it's out there, we just don't understand the nature of it. We suspect there are unknown subatomic particles involved and we hope to discover those here at LHC."

"What about gravity and dark matter?" Ben steps forward with keen interest.

So he's got a healthy inner nerd too... Yes! I smile to myself.

"Yes, that's an important force of nature... Yet in the world of subatomic particles, gravity has little influence because, in relative terms, it is so weak. It's really all about electromagnetism."

Ben whispers in my ear, "In my world, electromagnetism is really just kama."

"What's kama?" I look up at him.

"The tantric word for love," his eyes soften as he loops his hand through my hair another time; I think he is breathing me in.

"I love you" runs through my mind. I'm too shy to say it, but I smile to myself, thinking it, and am taken aback by new found sentimentality.

***

Electromagnetism and *kama*. Ben and I are sitting at the main CERN cafeteria discussing particle physics and love. There is a scientist sitting beside us working on her laptop, solitary and alternately chewing the eraser of her pencil and her thumbnail. There are clusters of physics graduate students huddled together in the sun. There are world leaders here too sitting in a room designated as 'the glass box'. Ben and I can see them there eating salad and talking. Our tour guide recommends that we should stay and eat because many of the most important discoveries of the project were formulated here in the cafeteria, not in the lab.

"Tim Berners-Lee and Robert Cailliau decided to name their project the World Wide Web over fish and beer at that cafeteria," he had said. "So many people pass through there. Nobel Prize winners, royalty, and people like us."

Ben and I have found a table in the sun on the terrace.

"The basis of human consciousness is desire," Ben is saying. "That and electromagnetism, these are fundamental actions in nature. I feel both so strongly when beside you."

The whole tour at CERN was a double-entendre, the laws of the universe and the nature of love fully interchangeable beside the giant particle collider. Ben was beside himself with glee, squeezing me with delight throughout the tour.

"Electromagnetic fields, by your logic, govern the actions of molecules and therefore govern the universe."

"Just like kama governs the actions of man."

"It's all just chemistry," I smile and stretch my arm across the table to caress Ben's neck. He's right, there is electricity here. It is undeniably real. His skin flushes at my touch. I have never allowed myself to engage in the world this way, the fun of sexually charged and playful banter. It's intoxicating here at this table with all of the scientists deconstructing the universe around us.

"The three D's affect everything—desire informs our decisions and ultimately our deeds."

I am called from my nature to add, "What about duty? It can't be just about pleasure all of the time."

"Kama isn't just about sexual pleasure, Ginny, it's about our duty to enjoy life's pleasures, whether it be sex, food, dancing, the feeling of the sun on the skin, your voluptuous kiss. People think that the *Kama Sutra* is a book about sex positions. In reality only about 1/4 of the book is about that, the majority of the book is about the philosophy of love and desire. How is it that you can accept electromagnetism so readily and doubt kama? What if part of your duty in the world, part of what makes the world a better place is our ability to create art, to read beautiful books, and to practice the art of making love?"

Something about the way he says making love melts me down to my knees. My cognition persists though.

"Art is a concrete thing, a book is a concrete thing, passionate love is this undefinable thing."

"Like electromagnetic waves. Yet undeniable?" he grasps my hand so fully and passionately that it takes my breath from me.

"Yes, undeniable," I say because it is true and because I can say nothing else.

We bathe a while in that silence that says more than the talking and slowly he leads me away from the table to a quiet and hidden place on the CERN campus and we make love, no shyness, no inner panic, no awareness of people, of past or of future. He just lifts the skirt of my romper, unzips his jeans, pulls my lower lips down with his thumb and enters me fully. We completely go with the sexual energy rather than fight against it. I wrap myself around him and allow myself to experience fully the flood of emotions and sensations as they build and gather into a full release. I slide my finger through the loop of his belt and let go. No thoughts, just him in me. I am fully undone, shattered into a million beautiful pieces, concurrent harmony and the Big beautiful Bang.

Chapter Twenty-Seven

"Whoever offers me with devotion, a leaf, a flower, a fruit or water, I accept that, the pious offering of the pure heart. Whatever you do, whatever you eat, whatever you offer in sacrifice, whatever you give away, whatever path you follow, do it as an offering to me," Ben is reading to me from the *Bhagavad Gita*.

We are home again. I am wearing one of his button up shirts like a robe and am resting my head in his lap. He is talking about sex as a form of devotion.

"According to tantra, all energy is divine, and there is no greater exchange of energy between humans than sex. It is both physical and spiritual."

His eyes are soft with a look of utter devotion, to me. And while there is a way in which I absolutely love it, there is another way in which it makes me want to run and hide. Ben can see me shifting side to side.

"Ginny, you know you are beautiful, right?"

I can't meet his eye. I laugh with discomfort and look down. He grasps my chin.

"You know you are beautiful, right?" he repeats.

My discomfort is this palpable thing right on the floor between us.

"You know that in order to fully love another person, you have to first love yourself?" He leans forward towards me. "Part of what is important about sex is that it brings all of this to the forefront, any self-loathing, guilt or embarrassment. It brings it all right here to the surface."

I look up at him and close my eyes and the tears roll down my cheeks. My body. Jacqui always pushed me in this way. She always wanted me to inhabit and nurture my body as much as my mind, but it has been a struggle to do so. The mind, I can handle. My body has been both over and sometimes underwhelming.

"Sometimes in political science women are taught to neutralize sexuality," I began my intellectual retort but then the tears just take over, "I mean, I just try not to look in the mirror."

"And the running…" he begins.

"It numbs me more," I close my eyes again.

Ben purses his mouth then bites his lip into a saddened expression, "Here, let's try this." He pulls a blanket from the couch and drapes it across the rug. "Lie down on the blanket. Get really comfortable, and close your eyes."

Great, something for me to do—directions. It comes as a relief.

"Perfect," he says, but I know he is talking about something else. I peer out from behind my tears and he is smiling over me, taking in every inch of me.

"Take seven deep and slow breaths, a count of four in, a count of four out."

I do as he asks. The tears quiet. My mind slows.

"Now I am going to touch you, very gently," he offers.

I nod. My whole body warms at the thought of his touch. I feel his hands fumble with the buttons of the shirt, one by one he pulls them free and the shirt falls open to the floor. For a long time there is just silence and I know that he is just looking at me. I can feel his eyes hungrily sliding up and down along my curves.

"Are you warm enough? I want you to be perfectly comfortable."

I nod, enjoying the very faint feel of his breath on my body.

"Now with your eyes closed I want you to imagine looking in the mirror at your naked body. And tell me what you see, how you feel. Start with your toes and move all the way to the top of your body."

I take a deep breath, "I see my toes. They are painted a pale violet. They are tanned from the sun. My feet are small. My baby toe is scrunched up along the edge of my foot...even when I try to uncurl it, it huddles right back up."

"Now breathe," he interrupts me and gently caresses my foot kissing every toe, worshipping the creases and folds. "And tell me about the other foot. How is it different from this one." I feel the heat of his breath on my foot as he speaks. It is so sexy.

"Well, the other one is my left foot. It is stronger than my right. It is my dominant foot. My lead foot, my soccer foot. There is a cluster of freckles, a secret constellation hidden behind my ankle."

Ben starts with the freckles, kissing every last one, then moves through the foot with equal precision and love.

"Tell me about your ankles." As he speaks he traces his finger along my ankle. And before I can begin, he is devouring them too with love and adoration. The sensation is so overwhelming that it is difficult for me to speak, waves of pleasure drift up and down my legs. He takes little love bites, nibbles my toes and ankles. It almost hurts, tickles, and sends waves of playful delight through my legs. There is something incredibly sexy about looking up to see him pay such attention to what is usually far below me, and not given much thought.

"Well, I've never really thought about my ankles. I guess they are angular and a little bit bony."

He traces the angles of my ankle with his tongue.

"They're strong," I say. "A lifetime of running and I've never sprained an ankle." I start to laugh because he is running his tongue up the inside of my leg and it tickles.

"Can you tell me about your calves?"

The heat that is building inside of me is almost unbearable. He starts to nip along the back of my leg. I start to mumble because I can no longer think of any words to say. It is all just sensation and adoration. He steps back and starts to trace the contours of my legs with his finger. His touch is so light. Then abruptly, the kissing begins again. He slides his tongue along my knee, up my thigh, arriving between my legs. He is kissing me softly. He is licking me and swirling his tongue in soft circles over my panties. I am getting so wet that I think he can taste me right through them. He offers deep groans of satisfaction and just when I think he is about to enter me, he moves up to my belly. Sweet torture. He spends a long time there massaging and loving my belly. He nips along the side of my buttocks to my waist. The higher he moves along my body, the more heat and quick the movements.

He cups my breasts with his hands. It is becoming hard to differentiate all of the sensations. The effect is dizzying.

"Ginny, what do you see?"

"I don't, I just feel."

"Nice. Describe what you feel."

"It's," my mind stalls out again. "You're my ambrosia. I feel intoxicated."

"Exactly," he says and captures my mouth in his.

He holds his hand on my heart, takes off my panties, and enters me slowly and we make love over and over again.

He's right, the journey is about seeing within yourself and to love myself better means to love him better.

Chapter Twenty-Eight

Our life has developed somewhat of a rhythm. We wake; we make love; we explore some new facet of Geneva; we eat and drink; we come home; we share a glass of wine and unwind; we make love again. I have fully disengaged from my life as I knew it, just for now, just for a while. We have been relaxing into each other, into the sexual energy, as tantra teaches, as Ben teaches me, and that focus and energy seems to permeate and color everything else—my inner and outer worlds. This sexual energy seems to give the rest of our life that same loving, relaxed ease.

I am reminded of coming upon Ben in the grass by the lake when I was running and noted how the figure in the distance seemed so at home in his body, exuded an agile grace, a serene sensuality. And now I feel I am closer to embodying this way of moving through the world. I don't know if this is just the "honeymoon" phase, and boy Jacqui was right, it is sweet as honey, but I'll take it. It feels so good. And today we are going to the Bain des Paquis, the 1930s swimming baths set along Lake Geneva.

"The best part is the people watching," Ben offers. "While eating fondue…"

Mmmmm, the thought of fondue, cheese and then chocolate, fills me with such anticipatory delight and hunger. The Bain de Paquis is surrounded by a beach and set on an artificial peninsula beside the jet d'eau. There are people draped across every surface. There are saunas, hammams, or dark rooms used for exfoliation, two turkish baths and a restaurant. Collectively, the facility is known as Les Bains des Paquis. Most people are naked. This part makes me nervous and uncomfortable.

When I express this to Ben he tells me impetuously, "You're a fanatic. We came into this world naked, you know, and we are in this life to enjoy it."

He is kissing my neck and undressing me. I promised him that if we came here I would bathe naked and I am sharing with him how I am starting to have second thoughts.

"You are radiant and yet you are hiding away the greatest gift you have to give to humanity."

"Well, I'm pretty sure I have other gifts to offer!"

"You know what I mean. Let your worries and concerns go for another day. You cannot fix Fredrick, you cannot fix the world, you can only fix what is within your own realm, and, in doing so, it benefits everything else. There is no virtue in misery. Don't make your life some martyrdom to misery," he pleads.

He is braiding my hair, which is an unfair tactic. We have been debating all morning, ever since I posed the question whether it was selfish to focus so much on engaging in our own pleasure and not to strive for other goods, like to make everyone's life this beautiful.

"Well, my friend, if I am a fanatic, then I must say you are a heretic and a hedonist," I smile as my last piece of clothing falls away from my body. Two can play at this game.

"If I am a heretic then I must ask for absolution or, better yet, please, please subject me to a life-long sentence of kama with you,

with your mind and soul, fully and with all of the facets of my
senses, my hearing, seeing, tasting, smelling and feeling. To love
you, I will do anything."

His words pierce through me, and my lower lip begins to
quiver just a little. I am, perhaps, equally as scared as I am in love.
I am scared to make a wrong move, to lose this love, to do
something to lose it or worse, just lose it for reasons unknown and
out of my control. And at the same time, I'm scared to let it fully
in and embrace it, because both feelings seem like two sides of the
same coin.

"You speak so freely of love; you are so at ease with all this,"
an involuntary tear falls from my cheek.

"I'm sorry, my love. Am I making you uncomfortable?"

"No, not at all. It's just so unexpected and beautiful."

"It's just, quite simply, how I feel. It's not rocket science. It's
pretty simple."

He kisses away my tears as we step into the bath together. For
him, I try desperately hard to forget that I am naked. He wants to
see me naked in the bright of day, and even more than that, he
wants me to feel sexy and confident while naked and in the light. I
am trying to inhabit that space—for him, for me, for us.

I pile my hair high on top of my head and lower into the water
slowly. Ben watches every inch of me all over and all at once with
that same intense serenity of the eye as it brushes up against a
sunset descending to the horizon. First the water envelops me with
great shivers and then Ben's arms encircle me. I feel his naked
form press against my back. I look around at all of the people
around us. They are oblivious to our universe of kama, distracted
by their own world. I still feel as though I am in a dream. I feel
loved and deeply desired; I feel like I love myself more; I feel
connection; I feel nearness, and yet I have this deep shuddering pit
in the deepest part of my belly that this is too good to be true, that

it is a mirage, that such an unfettered pursuit of kama might lead me to danger.

I turn away from that thought and pull him under the water with a kiss both ravenous and dizzying; skin on skin is the most sensuous way to float freely.

Chapter Twenty-Nine

"Passion is presence," Ben says to me. "Desire starts first as just a flicker." He lights the candle. "Then awareness. Be alert to that flicker of desire."

We are sitting on the grey rug with the cream swirl once again. It is dark and there is only a candle between us.

Flicker? I think to myself. The desire I feel for this man is more like an inferno.

"And when you feel it," he urges me, "relax into it." He smiles sweetly at me. "Watching the flame of the candle can help."

"According to tantra, sex is most pleasurable and powerful when you can relax into it, a sort of melting into one another."

I have never been known for my skills in relaxation. 'Stress case, driven, nervous, tense, jittery,' these are all words people could use to describe me. Tranquility is not a word or concept that I've ever explicitly striven for or even particularly valued. But things change. And sometimes, in spite of the odds, so do we.

"You have to get the energy in your body to relax and move downward so that it can move back upward with love making and orgasm. An important step, now bear with me, is to learn to relax

the pelvic floor." He smiles, "I love your pelvic floor by the way."
We laugh, and I am thankful for the light-hearted moment.

I ask him to tell me more about it.

"Well, we don't even realize it, but we tend to hold a lot of
tension in our pelvis. All the time, as we live our days. It
accumulates and doesn't serve us. Just the opposite. Tantra
teaches us to specifically and concertedly make an effort to release
the pelvic floor." He cups my pelvis, "release and relax into me.
Let the energy just move down into, and then out through my
hand."

At first I'm self-conscious, but then I decide to try in earnest.
Release into his hand. The sensation is quite remarkable. I note a
marked difference.

"Wow, I see what you mean."

"Yes, and you can practice it. Hold nothing there," and he
smiles again at me, "except me. Hold me gently, lightly…"

I feel myself sigh with relief as my body lets go, and with that
release, the tension my heart and head feel, loosens as well. I sigh
again. I have a feeling that I will be sighing a lot more in my
future.

Ben has brought out another book, *The Perfumed Garden*, an
Arabic sex manual, he reads,

"The languishing eye
Connects soul with soul"

For Ben, the opening begins with the eyes. He calls it soft
vision. I touch my belly and close my eyes. Once my body starts
to feel at rest, I open my eyes, slowly, slower than the sun rising
on the horizon. Instead of focusing on one thing, I let the images
surrounding me fall into my eyes, the candle, the silhouette of
Ben. It's a passive rather than active vision, a receiving of energy
rather than an exertion of energy. I can hear Ben's voice breathing
into my ear,

"Let go, soften" he says. "Relax more." He says again.

The energy of the desire takes hold. I feel it and follow it to Ben's body. He is resting on his side watching me with soft eyes. I gently nudge him to lie down on his stomach. I can feel this energy rising up his spine and so I lean down and trace his spine, vertebrae by vertebrae, with my tongue. I can feel the energy ascend as I do this. He rolls to the side. My tongue continues down his brow, his throat, his chest. He is stroking himself. My mouth takes hold, coaxing, massaging, licking his penis with my tongue. I can feel his energy intensify; he grows. Quickly I wrap my legs around him. I encircle him, our soft eyes gazing into each other. And it's really less the sensation than the vision, our eyes locked, we come together. He traces circles on my spine. I love him. I really love him.

***

For a long time after, we lay together, facing each other, soft, naked, warm limbs entwined. Ben smiles. Oh how I love that smile. He kisses me on the lips, then peppers me with kisses. His eyelash flutters mine.

"Are you giving me a butterfly kiss?" I ask in amused disbelief, "I haven't had or given one of those since I was a kid."

He laughs and does it again. Then he kisses my eyes. Then my nose. I laugh. It tickles. He nuzzles his nose against mine. We laugh. We are rubbing noses. He smiles.

"I love when you laugh like a kid," he tells me. He kisses me again, and I don't remember being this happy since I actually *was* a kid.

Chapter Thirty

The trains leave from Geneva every fifteen minutes, and from the photos it looks like something out of a fairytale. We are taking a train to Chillon, a castle along the shore of Lake Geneva at the foot of the Alps. It is Saturday, now fully three weeks after I fatefully ran out of the restaurant. So many things have changed. Like I've been reading for pleasure again, selecting books from Ben's bookshelf. I am beginning the Henry James' novella *Daisy Miller*, which, in part, is set in the Chillon castle. It is about an American girl named Daisy who travels to Europe and is courted and brought to the castle at Chillon by Winterbourne, an American raised in Geneva. His family disapproves of the match. For them, she is too American, too uncultured, too flirtatious, too uncultivated. I am only at the beginning of the story and it strikes a cord of fear in my heart. Her life is hampered by her own flirtatiousness with life, or rather, by the judgments of others' that those liberties and freedom draw.

Why do we value others' judgments of us so much that our own critical thoughts adopt these very fears and concerns? We give them power over, above, and to the detriment of our own desires and probable happiness. I ask myself, is this, what we are doing and feeling, Ben and I, respectable? Is it sustainable? What if Ben only loves me in this impermanent window of freedom, like some Peter Pan in Neverland? Am I his Wendy, his Daisy? What happens when this becomes real? Or worse, what if it doesn't?

Ben reaches out his thumb and smooths the worry crinkle of my brow, distracting me from my misgivings, as if he knows that I have unkindly thrown myself into doubt. He clasps his hands on either side of my face and kisses me,

"There's too much worry in your brow. No need, my love. I know I have found my one in a billion. I'm not a fool. I know what I've found in you and will not let you go."

My lips soften into his. These are the words I longed to hear. Ben is so good at drawing me out of my head and into my heart. He shifts me onto his lap. This is what he is so good at, holding me, bringing me back into the present, towards our senses, away from my deep ocean of uncertainty and into a sea of bliss. He pulls his head away and looks at my forehead where the creased lines of apprehension have just drifted away—for now, a respite. A calm returns to my countenance, which visibly pleases him. And I can feel him stir beneath me.

The train jostles side to side and I clasp the armrest beside me. He plays with my hair, softly breathing into the back of my neck as we arrive at the castle station. I absolutely love feeling his breath on my nape. I unconsciously tilt my head away, providing more nape room for his wants and will.

"We are at the castle, mademoiselle." He smiles.

"But Ben, what happens when real life begins again, when we're not at a fairy tale castle?" I toss the book at him playfully.

He looks at me. His eyes intense, illuminated, lustful, real. He clasps my hands together into his one hand. I look searchingly at him.

"This is real, Ginny. This is real life, right here and now. It doesn't get more real than this, than the present. We are in it."

***

The castle is surreal, over 100 structures fused together over time, history in the present. It is massive. Save for a visit to the Biltmore Estate in Asheville, North Carolina as a child, and a tour of some very posh summer homes in Newport, Rhode Island, I haven't much experience with old castle-like homes. Europe seems filled with them, and I am delighting in this one. We wander through some of the main rooms. They are great halls staged to look as they might have looked so long ago. There are bedrooms, courtyards and caves to wander through. I clasp Ben's hand tightly in mine, emboldened by his steady resolve. Unlike Fredrick, Ben is quick to smile. It is difficult to cross his humor, and he enjoys the simple pleasures of holding hands in the cave or the sunshine reflected across the water. I have come to realize how holding hands with someone you love can add a deliciously satisfying contentment to any moment.

"I am a fool for you Ginny," he looks down at me and smiles in a way that was not known to me, an emergence of something, like the incarnation of spring. It is alien yet so deeply stirring. Ben does not turn his head away from that sensation, the one that now rests humming along my skin like a hymn.

"Let's go all the way to the top," I say.

The castle is primitive and a little bit scary. The stairway to the top is dizzying, so we step carefully together. Although some rooms are staged, the castle is mostly bare, bold stripes and patterns line the wall. When we arrive at the top, we can see all the way down Lake Geneva. I feel a pang of vertigo. I squeeze Ben's hand and look into his eyes to anchor me. Like a magician's spell it takes over, that vast wilderness of love. I am so thankful that I now associate Lake Geneva with a luscious, lustful love. How the tides have turned.

***

We finish the day with a bath and a glass of wine. This is what Ben likes to do, unwind and connect at the day's end. Turns out it's what I like to do too. I grasp the edge of the tub with both hands and lower down. I am kneeling between his legs, facing him. He is watching me intently. His lips are pursed. His breath is still. I caress his face and lean in to kiss him,

"Thank you," I say.

"Ginny," he says. I watch his tongue move in his mouth as he speaks. He is so sexy.

I reach up and run my fingers through his hair. He closes his eyes. I lean in to bite his lower lip. I can tell he is happy by the way the soft skin along his neck flushes scarlet as he lets out a deep sigh of his own. I turn and nestle into his embrace, my back to his chest. I can feel him harden. He leans down and kisses the back of my neck. He bites my ear. I can feel his pulse. I lift my body and hover above him in the water until he fills me. I settle back into his lap, this time with him inside me. Our lovemaking has become wordless now, intuitive. Our breath links in. His hands gently cup my breasts. The warmth of the bath and the sensation of him so deeply inside of me is overwhelming. He is drawing circles around my breasts with his fingers. He is licking my neck. I am melting more and more. We are moving together. In no time, I am coming. I throw my head back and wrap my arms behind his neck.

"I love you, Ginny," he whispers, his words like nectar, ambrosia, the water swirling around us, and I know I love him with every ounce of my being.

"I love you too," I whisper and close my eyes.

After a moment of quiet, I speak up, "But you didn't come?"

Ben smiles so sweetly, "That's perfectly all right baby. It's good. It felt amazing, you felt amazing. I was so pleasured, and

now we can enjoy each other again tonight. I look forward to it."
I'm a bit taken aback, and just not used to it. Sensing that, he
continues. "I don't need to come each time. Not at all. The
energy is key, the connection, the being naked with you, close to
you, kissing you, being inside you. It stirs me so. That was
beautiful with you. Coming is great, don't get me wrong, but it's
not a goal, not for me. Being with you, intimate and close, that's
what's so important, so needed, so wanted."

"You are amazing," I say and mean it wholeheartedly.

The water settles around us. The apartment is quiet. I am
exhausted and peaceful and so happy that I'm again a tad fearful,
because I really don't ever want to lose this.

***

As we lay in bed, embraced, I can't help wonder, "Why me?"
Why out of all the women in the world, would Ben choose me? It
is so clear to me that I have fallen head over heals in love with
him and it is just so obvious to me why I have. But his reasons for
doing so with me are not nearly as understandable to me—they
remain opaque even in the face of his sweetly trying to put them
into words and hand them over to me. My insecurities rear their
medusa heads yet again. There are so many far more beautiful
women than me, there are smarter, wealthier, more talented
women. So why? Why does a man ever choose a particular
woman? We most likely will never know these answers. They are
so specific, so intrinsic. But I also know that it's these things, these
insecurities that weasel their way into my consciousness, that
wreak havoc. I try not to let these thoughts have their way, but
rather trust in the attraction that so miraculously occurs. But they
do keep popping up.

Just when I'm lost in thought about all the things that could
wrong, Ben rolls over and kisses me. His weight on me feels so

good. Just the pure heft seems to soothe me. I put my hands around his arms. Those muscles! I am starting to dream about Ben's arms, missing them when I'm not feeling them, not with him, and reaching for them when I am.

Ben is looking directly into my eyes. You only see his smile lines around his eyes when he is truly smiling and you are up close and personal. I gently touch and kiss them. I love this part of him so much.

"I love your smile immensely," Ben responds. And I realize I am in turn smiling as big as he is.

He elaborates, "I love your million dollar smile" and then his mischievous boyish look appears, "and your multi-million dollar ass."

"Hey!" I hit him with a pillow. "You can't say that. You are supposed to be Mr. Tantric. That's so objectifying."

"Well I may be 'Mr. Tantric,'" he laughs, "But I'm still a man, I'm still human. And you, my dear, happen to have a very gorgeous ass."

I sit up and move a bit away. I don't know what to make of this conversational turn. It's not the kind of thing I usually approve of, but I'm glad that Ben finds me so attractive. That's a good thing.

"Ginny, have you ever thought of being thankful? You have such a beautiful body, so you don't have to spend any unnecessary effort or time thinking about it. That's a real gift. So many people in this world spend such an inordinate amount of time worrying about such things. But you can use all that extra energy for other things....like doing good in the world, and for now, I think the best good you can do is to bring that gorgeous ass right back over here!"

Chapter Thirty-One

It's been such a wonderfully epicurean few weeks; Ben's sensuality is downright prodigal in nature. But my "sensible" and by this I mean "pragmatic" side is starting to get concerned that this frivolity is just too much. Can there be too much of a good thing? I am so used to working and being slightly anxious about getting everything accomplished and meeting everyone's expectations and needs around me, that basking in the light of a gorgeous man, spending days hiking, visiting castles, viewing art in the likes of the beautiful Musee Arianna, kissing and making love all of the time, is a totally new experience. And anything the slightest bit new can set me off feeling anxious, even when what is new is as utterly delightful as this. Someone once told me that's just how we are made, any change, good or bad, can feel unsettling—even Herculean—just because it's the unknown. We get so very comfortable with what we know. I must have somewhat of a grimace on my face, because Ben turns to me and asks, "What's wrong Ginny? You look worried."

"It's nothing"

"I don't believe you. Your body seems tense to me."

"Well I'm just not used to this…"

"To what?"

"To whatever it is we've been doing."

"I believe it's called falling in love. Or do you mean you're not quite sure about the opening up to each other in the moment and really living according to your heart for once?"

"Yeah, that. I'm not sure about that." We both smile.

"You're not sure about being receptive towards grace, and making yourself more aware of the beauty in the moment that surrounds you?"

"Well when you put it like that!" We laugh. "But seriously, I know we keep coming back to this conversation. But I'm trying to work out why all of this wonderfulness makes me feel a bit uneasy. I think maybe I am just more concerned with making everyone else's life better. Why should I dwell in the beauty of a moment when so many suffer? Isn't it more splendid to help others, to better others' lives? That is what is both beautiful *and* meaningful to me."

Ben had a kind but determined look in his eye as he replied, "I respectfully disagree. I think the best piety we can do is to be aware of and appreciate what is in front of us at every turn. This is what we have. This, right now, is what is most real. The rest is fantasy. I think that if we all allowed ourselves to actually enjoy and be present in the moment, to actually *allow* ourselves to be happy, it would be the greatest gift to everyone. Your happiness would radiate into the world."

I'm still somewhat unconvinced, "But is that *really* what the world needs—my radiance and happiness? What would get done? What about the people who have nothing to enjoy, no beauty to speak of around them? What about shedding light for those in darkness? I think the world needs my effort, my work, *more* than it needs my happiness."

"That's really what you think the world needs? A bunch of drones working like worker bees for the queen? That's what's going to make the world a better place? Why martyr yourself? Where does this fanatical empathy of yours come from? Why willingly commit to your own doom? What on earth would compel you to do that? Sorry for all the questions, but I'd really like to know. It seems to me when the stakes are this high, the questions should at least be asked, if not answered thoughtfully and wisely."

Dang it, he has a point. I've never really thought through my position. But perhaps it really is just my nature. And I wonder if I can do other than my nature? Can any of us?

Ben continues, his exasperation beginning to stir, he is taking this seriously, taking me seriously; "It makes me sick to my stomach to think of you living out your days working away in a cold library, a veritable tomb beside Fredrick who can't see past the beaked nose on his stupid face. I always thought he was an idiot, but can recognize, work wise, he has done a lot for me—or at least he thinks he has. But Ginny, honestly, the fact that Fredrick is willing to make your life worse than it could and *should* be, to implicate you into his small miserable life is simply unforgivable to me. He should know better than that. If that's how he wants to live his life, fine, that's one thing, but to lure you into it….that's just too much. And that you are *willing* to follow him down that path, submitting to what you don't even like or love; that's killing me. Ginny, thinking of your beautiful lips kissing that cold mouth—I could punch him in the face. I watched you grow paler and thinner by the day when you were caught up in his lair. Please Ginny, I personally would much rather you be happy than miserable. You would do *me*, personally, a great service to enjoy your life. Now *that* would be a service."

I feel so confused. What is he talking about? I hear his words, and they resonate through my soul, as if he is speaking aloud and putting to words all my internal confusions, but ouch…this goes against everything I am, everything that somehow I've been taught, although I'm not sure by whom and when or why, exactly.

"Live a little Ginny. You are such a grown up. Have you ever even been a kid?"

I don't say anything. I look down, stunned. No one has said such things to me, ever. When I look up, Ben looks a bit sheepish. He takes my shaky hand.

"I'm sorry. I didn't mean to go off on you like that. My apologies...I didn't mean it to sound so condemning and condescending, I just *really,* really want you to be happy. It's something I think about *a lot.*"

I feel like he has painted me with the wrong brush. "But I am happy. I am not a melancholy person. That is not me."

I pause hearing those words come out of my mouth, that is how I see and experience myself, but I also can't help but remember how tear streaked my cheeks have been of late...including in front of Ben, and I'm not sure my words will ring true to him.

"I mean, yes, what you describe has been me of late. But it is not me *by nature.* That is me *by circumstance*...bad circumstances— at the moment—it is momentary, as you're so fond of saying. I promise you I am never unhappy for long. I'm a big girl. I take care of myself. Always. I've always had to. Make no mistake, I will figure this out. No matter how dark it is at the moment, how rainy or cloudy, there is always light and a rainbow near."

Ben smiles, "I'm glad to hear that, and I utterly concur. And I really respect and admire this part of you, this sublime strength you have. But Ginny, why do you always have to take care of yourself? Why can't you let me do some of that? Can you also please let me make you happy?"

Ben stops speaking. His last words reverberate through my whole being. We sit in the silence, looking into each other's eyes. I lean my head against his chest. He puts his arms around me. What is there to say? I have never heard kinder words spoken.

***

If I were in a different place, I would have taken offense at some of Ben's sentiments. But as he spoke, I heard the feeling behind his words. He cares. His anger at my situation is because he actually wants me to be happy. That is his main concern. What a freaking foreign concept that is. Who in my life gets angry if and when I'm not happy? Maybe Jacqui, that's as close as it gets, but in truth, as much I love her, she is more concerned about her own happiness on any given day; which is as it should be. A deep sense of gratitude fills my body, pervades my blood, each cell, as I think of Ben's earnest sentiments for my well-being. Someone is looking out for my happiness. All of a sudden, I want to dance in the streets.

Chapter Thirty-Two

Okay, now I am really scared. I am most certainly in love with Ben, but as much pleasure as I have experienced, I worry that it won't last and now that I've tasted it, I can't imagine going back to being without it. I'm also starting to feel badly about not being in touch with Fredrick, and for not dealing with the situation at hand. I haven't even been checking my email, afraid of what might lie in wait for me.

"What do you think Fredrick is thinking right about now?" I ask Ben.

"Who cares? He's probably thinking something obnoxious. You know, a very good portion of the time, I just want to tell that guy where to shove that skinny..."

"Please don't say mean things about Fredrick. It's beneath you."

"It's not beneath me. Sorry. And it's even worse than that, now that I'm in love with you, I have to restrain myself even more. It had already been a colossal task to hold my tongue most of the time. You know what Ginny, I might as well tell you. I can't stand the way he treats most women, and most of all, I really couldn't stand the way he spoke to you. It was awful. It was rude, inconsiderate, and made him look like a total asshole. When he spoke to you, I would think 'he has no idea what he has and how to treat her.' It made my insides turn."

I know what he means. My stomach would twist and turn too, and I'd feel so ill at ease and upset when Fredrick spoke rudely to me. Especially in public. But I sometimes wondered if I was just being too sensitive. Seems like Ben doesn't think so.

But my optimism makes me go on, "Please, it can't be that bad. I know he can be a curmudgeon, and a misogynist, geez, I can't believe I'm saying this about someone I almost married, but at least he's an excellent scholar."

"Oh please, Fredrick's work is a joke."

I am taken aback, like I just got sucker-punched.

"What? How can you say that, he is considered a top scholar in his field!" A loyalty in me tries to move away from this conversational turn, but a dedication and stronger loyalty to myself encourages me to listen to what Ben has to say.

Ben retorts, "Top in his field by whom? By those who are impressed with his work ethic and productivity? Fredrick cares more about the quantity of his publications than about the quality of the work. I would think that you, as much as anyone, would care about whether it actually ever helps anybody. But the worst is that he takes other people's work and makes it his own—he co-opts people's ideas. I've seen it again and again. He combs through the literature and finds an idea, an original one, original to someone else, and incorporates it into his dull, detailed, own manuscript. He is an armchair political scientist. He is not in the world; he is stuck in other people's heads. There's no originality there. Now *your* work has originality."

I think I must look both horrified and mortified, because Ben back-peddles so quickly and reaches for my hand, "Sometimes I speak too strongly and too hastily. I know this about myself. Some

people don't like that about me. I don't particularly like it about
myself. I'm sorry."

But I get the feeling that Ben has thought a lot about this and
was only speaking aloud what had gone through his mind a
million times. I don't know how to respond; no rejoinder awaits
me. Then the weight of Ben's words hit me; is Fredrick's
remarkably steadfast work ethic really just in vain? That would be
utterly intolerable. A substantial part of my reason for being with
Fredrick was to help him with his good works. Is it true that his
work is not his own? It would be one thing to be with someone
who worked day and night, ignoring you and your relationship,
but with results that actually made the world a better place. It
would be entirely another thing to stand beside one who works all
the time for naught. That seems more selfish than not working at
all. And even sadder, it means in some ways, Fredrick is actually a
failure. It occurs to me: Fredrick probably even knows it! And
maybe, just maybe, that is why he acts like he does. It's all making
more sense and naively, it's just dawning on me for the first time.

"Ginny, I'm just pointing out facts. Does it actually matter
this much to you, whether Fredrick is *authentically* successful?"

"Yes, actually it does! And I thought by now you would
realize that about me, the way someone spends their time, and the
work that they do, really matters!"

I have to go get some air. This train of thought is very
unsettling. In some ways, the fact that Ben is the one to point it all
out to me makes it even worse. I decide to go for a run. What else
can I do? I tell Ben I need some air and space but that I'll be back
soon. I need to clear my head, and my heart. He looks hurt, but I
have to go.

***

As I'm running along lake Geneva, my thoughts race faster than my steps. Everything is gnawing at me. I try to decipher what this aching feeling is alerting me to. What is the feeling in my abdomen trying to say?

It occurs to me that I feel like I'm also mad at Ben, but I'm not sure why. Is it just because he is the messenger? That would not be fair. As I run, it starts to hit me, at least Fredrick works at something. I think back to my conversation about Fredrick's childhood, and get a flash of little Fredrick trying so badly to please his mother. At least he is decisive. Look at how he asked me to marry him. Which is worse, a perverse perseverance for naught or someone who points out others' failures without fully getting in the game himself?

For all of Ben's criticisms of Fredrick, it seems to me that Ben might be so afraid of failure that he doesn't truly put himself out there, at all. He doesn't even take the risk. Maybe Fredrick has a point, maybe Ben should work a little harder? I mean what does he actually want to do with his life? Is he ever going to finish his own dissertation, become a professor? It seems while he is so immensely critical of Fredrick, he still took Fredrick up on his offer of a research assistantship. And he's been doing it for four years! That's a long time to work with someone you neither respect nor like. What does it say about Ben that he spends his precious life "moments" doing that? And in the weeks we've been together we haven't worked at all.

I mean the sex is great and all—ok the best I could ever imagine, but can that sustain me? Can it be all pleasure and sex and not have the work take some precedence? I'm not Jacqui.

Chapter Thirty-Three

Returning to the apartment, Coltrane is playing. The music wafts through the small space. I love how Ben fills the air with music. The blinds are half-open and the sun is going down. I notice how the darkness in Ben's room is soothing. A completely different kind of darkness, a protective one. Ben has done something so that it smells nice in here too, incense, a candle? All my senses are soothed at once. Upon hearing me enter he comes to the door to greet me. He looks forlorn, which gives me a pang of remorse.

Ben says to me, immediately without pause, "I upset you; I'm so sorry. That's never my intention, just so you know."

"It's ok. Sometimes when people say things I don't want to hear, I get upset and feel the need to get away, quickly. It's not my best quality, but I do come around. I'm sorry if my leaving hurt you."

"No, it's my fault. I made things unpleasant and that's the last thing I want to do. I want to bring light and goodness into your life."

I lean over to kiss him, "You do; you are very kind to me."

While I am still confused, I am grateful for the charitable and loving things he says to me. These are no small things.

"I want to be more kind. I want to be able to be as kind to you everyday and every night as I possibly can. I want to love you with every sunrise, and every sunset. I fear only that you or circumstances won't let me."

I kiss him gently on those ever soft lips.

"Can I ask you a favor Ben? Can we not vilify Fredrick? I don't want that to happen. I don't want that to be a part of this...I know in part it is, but it doesn't feel right or good like that."

"I will try to hold my tongue. But it won't be easy."

He has a smirk with that last part, but realizes I am serious.

"Sorry, yes. I'll try. But if I don't speak it aloud, am I still allowed to think it, even more so in my head, to make up for the moratorium on speaking it aloud? Sorry, just kidding."

"Funny how people always say 'just kidding' precisely when they are not."

Ben thankfully laughs and we decide to let it go.

"I feel the need for re-connection. Let's make love," he says and takes my hand in his.

"I'm not sure I'm in the mood. I so appreciate all you've said and all you do, but I just don't feel that good right now."

"All the more reason. There is no better medicine for when you don't feel good or connected, than making love."

I wonder if he is joking. Is this really his philosophy—sex makes everything better—or is he just really horny?

"Seriously Ginny. I'm not just some teenage boy, if that's what you're thinking, but you'd be surprised what making love can do to change one's mood around. It can work wonders. Trust me. Let's give it a try. If it's not working for you, we can stop. I'm not just being self-serving, promise."

His smile still makes me question; I am very uncertain about this Tantric principle, but decide to give it a try. I let my worries wash away with a warm shower and return to find Ben naked and waiting for me on our bed.

He kisses me and my body starts to yield. I sink into his arms. His kiss feels sweet and sacred. Thoughts of Fredrick fade away to nothing.

Ben lays me on the bed. He kneels by my feet at the bottom of our bed. I look up at his statuesque torso, he takes my toe in his mouth. I squirm with the tickle of it. He sucks each toe and presses his tongue into the groove between. A luscious pain shoots through. He massages my calf and kisses it gently.

"You have the most beautiful legs."

He makes his way up my thighs with his tongue. As he reaches my sweet spot, he moans, "Ah this delicious wetness...I love how wet you get. This is my ambrosia".

I laugh, "You are always stealing my lines!"

But I secretly love that he adopts my words. It feels so intimate, so attentive, so loving.

He lays on top of me, lavishing me with warm gentle kisses. I reach down and feel he is soft; he starts to harden in my hand. I reach between his legs as he kisses me, his strong legs, and I massage his testicles. It's a foreign feeling for me and I am enjoying exploring them in my hand, and how he stirs when I do. He moans; I am, gratefully, learning all his pleasure noises.

He starts to harden more but he is not fully erect. He places himself inside me. This is new; here he is inside me, softer than I've experienced. He is quiet, his hands roving my body lovingly, and his kiss gets deeper and more passionate. I feel him get harder inside me as his tongue swirls the inside of my cheek. It's so sexy, our lips' embrace and the feel of our naked bodies together is stirring his arousal. I am feeling all the effects, moment by moment. Now he is fully hard and lifts himself up. His graceful chest hovering above me; he looks down and then into my eyes, his sweet smile lines so apparent at this proximity.

Still inside me, he twists me to my side, seamlessly. We are moving in unison, as one. I am not quite sure of his position, is he kneeling? He is holding my left thigh up and his other arm is around my waist. I feel him between me. He gives me time to enjoy this particular angle, and then he turns me again. This time onto my stomach. And he takes me from behind as I'm on my hands and knees. I can't see him. But oh lordy, I can feel him. With each rotation I experience him inside me differently. We are exploring all the ways we fit together, a perfect puzzle.

On my knees, then sitting on his lap, my back against his stomach, my thighs on his thighs, he touches me gently, playfully as I raise and lower myself.

"Ginny...." he cries out and he buries his face in the nape of my neck as he comes.

At the end of making love, spooning each other, Ben behind me, his thighs against mine, his gorgeous chest on my back, his lips gently kissing my back, his arm wrapped around me, his hand resting so lovingly on my breast, he says, "welcome back" and I know he means welcome back to my body, to peace, to love, to connection. My worries completely faded, as my body took over, and I was one with him and myself again.

Oh my stars, did that ever work!

I tell Ben, "I feel like a different person. I should listen to you more often."

"I agree totally," Ben replies and we lay in each other's arms, reconnected, and content.

After a little while, I have to ask, "Is tantra really this simple? We just make love and it makes things all better?"

"I think so. And it's not rocket science. Amazing isn't it, how far away we've come from the answers, from the utter simplicity of what actually makes us happy? It's connection. And how are we ever more connected than we just were, than this, now?"

I feel so much gratitude, "I'm so glad I found you."

"Me too," he says, oh so lightly kissing my forehead.

Chapter Thirty-Four

We decide to go out on the town, leave our abode, and get
some fresh air. And besides I need to find a present for Jacqui for
her birthday. We head to Rue de Rhone; as we walk along I spy
the designer lingerie shop *La Perla* and think how Jacqui wouldn't
blink twice before excitedly skipping on into the racks. Ben looks
ecstatic as he quietly walks in behind me. His grin as I hold the
door is huge. He is a kid in a candy shop, quiet as a mouse, almost
as if he's scared that if he says anything, I'll change my mind, turn
around and leave.

As we go from display to display, Ben remains silent, his eyes
getting wider. I find a pale grey silk and lace slip, just enough lacy
fabric to cover the main parts, hug the others, and reveal a lot. A
tease of a thing, but still very pretty. I hold it up to get a better
look.

"Perfect," Ben says "Absolutely perfect. Let's take it home
now."

I laugh, "Oh no, I could never pull this off. But Jacqui will
rock it!"

"I think *you* would look *amazing* in that. Tell you what, you
get one for your sister, and I'll get a matching one for you." Ben's
smile reminds me of the proverbial cat that ate the canary.

"I can't wear that!"

"Oh yes, you certainly *can*." He looks both so mischievous and desirous.

Could I do this for Ben? Wear this? Do I need to? Doesn't that go against what I believe in? Why should a woman wear garments that do such things to her body—push this up and this other down? Even this one, without the wires—I mean *wire* for crying out loud— looks fairly uncomfortable, like you'd be pulling it down here but up there. Why are such accoutrements needed to be sexy? Isn't the female form sexy enough, as is, naturally, without being tamed and trimmed and altered in this way and that? I've never understood the fetishism of lingerie or of the female body for that matter. I just haven't bought or played into that fantasy. Jacqui calls my underwear "granny pants," which they are not! I think they are normal, pretty, graceful, but comfortable underwear, even with a hint of lace. Thus far I've rather taken a stand, and been very comfortable doing so. I mean men's underwear seems perfectly reasonable. Heck, I'd love to wear boxer briefs everyday. That would be perfect.

But for Ben? Is this what he means by my opening up to his desires as well as opening up to mine? I don't really think so, but his look makes me ever more aware that he is getting quite turned on. I attempt to change the subject.

"Jacqui and I have never been apart as long as this."

I watch him walk over to the cash register.

"Done."

***

Following my afternoon run, I call Jacqui to wish her happy birthday, it's so good to hear her voice.

"Awww. Thanks for calling Gigi. It is a happy birthday indeed. But how are you? It's been a while and I really want to know."

I decide as part of her present, in addition to the sexy lingerie, I'll let her know about Ben. The two go together after all. I tell her what happened in the restaurant and how Ben and I have been 'getting to know each other.'

"That's amazing Gigi. Fredrick deserves it. Ben sounds super yummy. And how's the sex?"

"It's part of everyday life now. I never saw it like that before. It's like there is always a fire burning within me. And sometimes, we just add more wood."

Jacqui cracks up.

"'Ha ha,' I know it sounds funny, but really I mean it. It's like we're always ready at a low slow burn, glowing embers, tinders ready to be stoked and ignited more. Then when it happens, I am fully ablaze. I mean not all the time, of course. But much more often than I ever thought would be the case."

"Dang Gigi, you're getting me all heated and fired up just listening to you!"

We laugh, "fired up," I really am finally understanding language.

I pause. I know this conversation will be an added birthday present for Jacqui.

"The sex itself is exquisite, but honestly, what really, really gets me is the foreplay and afterplay. Now those are amazing."

"What?" Jacqui sounds beyond herself excited. "What is afterplay?"

We are both laughing that, for once, I am, the one to shed light on a sexual matter. That has never happened before. This is a first.

"It's all the great stuff that happens after making love."

"Dang girl, give me an example!"

"Well yesterday afternoon, after a two-glasses of wine lunch followed by a two orgasms for me, love making session, Ben was still on top of me, and we were just kissing each other gently. We were looking into each other's eyes and smiling like teenagers but also like a couple celebrating their 50th anniversary and as in love as the day they met, or even more so because of all they've been through together. We very slowly and sleepily fell asleep, naked in each other's arms. Ben on top of me. We fell asleep holding each other. We could feel each other's sleep shivers and would wake each other up with them, and smile and kiss and go back to a light slumber. It was so sexy. We were as close as can be, two as one. That was yesterday's afternoon afterplay. It was as delicious as all that came before."

"No way! Wait, two-glasses of wine at lunch and sex in the afternoon! Two orgasms? Who is this? I demand you put my sister back on the phone immediately!" Jacqui laughs and I know she heartily approves.

"I know! Honestly it's so good, does anything good last? Nothing gold can stay, right?"

But even as happy as I know this conversation is making her, I feel she is unusually ecstatic sounding. I hear something else in Jacqui's voice, an even more heightened excitement than usual, and it's not just because of the 'after play' discussion.

"Jacqui, what's going on with you? Spill." My sisterly love and concern is gushing forth so strongly that all my troubles vanish in an instant. It's a good feeling. I love her so much that when she is happy, I feel happy.

"Oh Ginny, I don't know what to say. You've been gone so long. Our place felt so lonely when you left, and so Evan started coming over more, to keep me company. And me him. He said he missed you a lot. You were always such a companion for him."

"This sounds serious."

"And Ginny," there was a long, unusual pause, "I really, really like him, I'm going to ask him to move in, if that's ok with you. Assuming you're gonna be gone for a while with Fredrick and all...or actually with Ben. Ben! So cool! That makes me so happy. I really did not like Fredrick, I'm just gonna say it."

I don't want the focus to return to me, because this sounds serious.

"Wow, Jacqui, are you in love? It's not like you to get serious like this."

"Yes. I think I am," I hear a little squeal. "But I want to take it slow. I really think Evan is the one, Gigi, and he says the same. But I know that when you're married, it's for a very long time... So I want to take our time, do things, explore, live a little, not married. Really make sure. Why not? If it's true love, there is plenty of time."

This sounds like my sister invaded by a foreign being. She sounds so very ...reasonable. I am starting to think that maybe she does better in the world when I'm not around. And possibly that I have underestimated her, and while so doing, overestimated my own judgment.

"Hey. Whoever this is, put my sister back on the phone."

Jacqui laughs. "Seriously, What do you think Gigi?"

"Well, Jacqui, I think it doesn't get better than Evan. He's hard working and he's good fun. And most importantly," it was my turn to pause, "he's kind. Very kind."

"Gigi, I know you think he might not be as educated as Fredrick. But I don't need a world-renowned scholar."

My heart stops for a moment. Had I made it so apparent how highly I placed intellectual pursuits over other things, like kindness and love? Ugh. I ponder a moment to think how my own criteria have not necessarily served me so well in my own search for love.

"My goodness, Evan is one of the smartest men I know. Look who he is choosing to be with. Doesn't get any smarter than that."

"Thanks Gigi, that means a lot. I know it would mean a lot to him too. He thinks so highly of your opinion. I love you, sis."

"I love you too, sis. I really miss you. More soon, ok."

"Yes, definitely."

As I hang up, I think about the world, and the people in it. I feel a bit lost.

***

Following my conversation with Jacqui, my thoughts turn to Evan and Fredrick and how incredibly different they are. I don't know why I dwell on this particular comparison. We are all different after all, but sometimes it's interesting to articulate how. For example, Evan pays much more attention to his own health and body. At first, in my friendship with Evan, I found that to be vain, but now as I witness Fredrick's lack of concern in that arena, I wonder if it's not more important than I realized. Fredrick devoted his days to a life of the mind, over the body. I admired that at one time. I still do. But the body is important. It's our home. Ben is showing me that, actually. Ben's relationship to his body is inspiring. It's not vain, but he's so gorgeous. He seems to view and inhabit his body as a vessel from which to connect to others and the world, and thus he needs it to be as sharp and open, as ready as it can be, for the best connection to be made. Oh my, who am I? I sound like I have been indoctrinated. Well, maybe it's a good indoctrination. I thought Fredrick would show me the world. His world was barren. But Ben, it's a whole new world out there, or rather, as I think of my own body and mind, Ben would remind me, in here.

I decide to call Jacqui back. Maybe she can give me some advice.

***

"Hey! What's up sis. You again?" I can hear her smile through the phone. How lovely to have someone sound so gleeful to hear your voice on the other end of the line, even when you just hung up a moment ago.

"Oh Jacqui, I don't know what to do. I'm pretty sure Fredrick is not right for me."

"Well what about Ben? He sounds to die for, or rather, and even better, to live for."

"He is. But I don't truly know where I stand with him. He seems so amazing, but also like a fantasy. I'm not sure if he's real; I'm not positive his feelings for me are real or sustainable, and I'm not sure what a life with Ben would actually look like, in the real world."

"But Gigi, I'm pretty sure you're in the real world. Or am I missing something? And if it means anything, Evan said he didn't take to Fredrick from the very beginning, that he didn't give you half enough attention and adoration as we, Evan and I, think you deserve. Evan is so matter of fact about these things, you know. He says Fredrick should be thanking his lucky stars just to sit across from you for one meal, let alone anything else. He says most men would do anything to have that opportunity, that most guys would flip burgers all day if it meant coming home to you, and that you are downright sacrificing yourself. He still is really kind of mad about it. For a long time after you left, that's mainly what we talked about. It drove me a bit bats, but I also think it's really sweet. He thinks we should do everything possible so that you don't marry Fredrick; that you deserve a much better fate."

I feel frozen, my stomach twists and I feel downright sick to hear these thoughts so clearly stated by another. My heart feels parched.

"What do you say, Jacqui, when Evan says those things?"

"I tell him I feel exactly the same but that you never have acted according to public opinion, so why would you start now? I remind him how you've always made your own way and, in truth, often surprise me in your choosings."

We have a laugh. She does get me. I do miss her. And Evan is so sweet. I used to think he may have had feelings for me at one point, ones that if he did, were unrequited on my part, but he has never shown any bitterness, only tenderness and caring toward me. Jacqui is the right choice for him. She will do very well by him, and he her.

When I hang up, I recognize that Fredrick has not done right by me for a long time and that I just need to tell him so and end it. Ben is teaching me the importance of embracing the moment, how to not turn away from both pain and pleasure. With Ben, I have learned so much about the importance of letting in pleasure. Making time and room for the lingering, sensual and joyful aspects of life, the taste of dark chocolate on my tongue, the pleasure of waking up slowly to the aroma of coffee, a passionate kiss in the middle of the afternoon. And we have planned a lovely evening together tonight. I take a deep breath. Fredrick can wait.

I think of Ben's excitement from the morning. He is always thinking of my pleasure and well-being, but it can't just be about me. I grab my purse and decide to go back to the lingerie store. I saw which items his eyes were drawn to; the silky feel of a slip can be just as stimulating as *The Odyssey*. It doesn't have to be a choice *between* brain and body. Both matter.

Chapter Thirty-Five

It tickles me just to walk through the lingerie shop's threshold again. This time I feel more empowered. I let go of some of my more political concerns. Women are amazing. We can be strong and sexy in myriad ways. I'm starting to understand this more deeply, for myself. My understanding of women's power is growing more capacious. Everyone can do it in their own way, but I'm going to embrace this way, for now, by trying on this blue and yellow satin slip.

This is a good thing to be doing. It's something unusual for me. Everyone used to say in college to step out of your comfort zone. Well, this is pretty darn far out of mine.

As I try on the negligee, I can sense myself glowing, alight with the thoughts of the night to come. Images and thoughts of giving Ben pleasure, bending this way and that way, the satin clinging to my curves, and Ben's eyes growing larger by the minute, spark my desire. I even think of dancing for him. Just a little, as he watches. Who has taken over me?

I look in the mirror. Yup, this will do. I see myself through his eyes, knowing that later he will do everything in his power to get me into my body, wholly, fully and then get into my body, wholly, fully. I take a moment in the dressing room just to ponder what he is doing to me and how being in this relationship, if I can call it that—yes, I can—is affecting me so strongly. It's quite wonderful.

I make my way to the register to pay for the garment. The woman behind the table smiles at me. "Good to see you again."

"Thank you," I say. "Good to be back." And for once I don't think I am blushing.

The woman pauses as she wraps my slip up in tissue paper. She asks in a tenuous tone, "Do you mind if I ask you a rather strange and personal question?"

"Not at all," I say as I am feeling more invincible than vulnerable for once.

"What's your secret? You look so notably happy, so alive. I've been feeling so 'blah,' lately. I really want to make changes in my life to be more fulfilled. And you radiate fulfillment. You seem to have the answers. I know it sounds weird, but if you don't mind, please tell me your secret. I want to be as happy as you look."

I am shocked a) that someone can tell and b) that I finally look happy. Ben would be ecstatic to hear this. I'll tell him tonight. But I don't know how to answer her obviously sincere query. I try, though, because she is asking in earnest.

"I am happy. I'd normally say finding good work is the key. And I do think it's important. But this smile that you are seeing, this is when someone awakens your heart. And you are excited just at the thought of seeing him or her next. You glow from having just been with your love and you await the next chance. You are embers waiting to be blown on. That's all I can say. But do it, go for it, find it. You can; you will."

She smiles, "I'll keep trying. I think I'll leave this job, too." She bends down and whispers, "Boss not so great." Then more loudly, "And I'll be open. Thank you for sharing. I know it probably seemed like an odd question."

"It's a great question. What's more important?" I hear myself ventriloquating Ben's words. "All we can do is be open to it. Open that door…"

I leave the store pondering how incredibly lucky I am at this moment. I know life is made of good and bad, happy and sad times, and given the givens the other shoe is sure to drop soon, as it always inevitably does, but for now, I'll take it. This, I'll totally take.

Chapter Thirty-Six

That night after dinner, I go into the bedroom and put on my new lingerie. When I come out into the living room, Ben has two flutes of perfectly sparkling champagne, one in each hand. His jaw drops and his eyes open wide. I love how expressive he can be. So gorgeous.

He sets the glasses on the table and moves closer. His strong hands go to my hips. He feels the slip, this way and that, following the fabrics' lines in all their directions and folds.

"This is beautiful. You are so sexy. Thank you."

"I'm glad you like."

"I love."

He takes my head in his hands and kisses me. His tongue enters my mouth. I breathe and release, conscious that my mouth is a soft warm, inviting place for his tongue to explore, as are other places. We kiss for a long time.

I tell Ben, "Sometimes I think that kissing you is my favorite part. Even better than sex. Don't get me wrong, I *love, love, love,* making love with you, but the kissing is just so incredible. It's like I can taste contentment itself in the tenderness of your lips. It makes me want to kiss you all the time."

When Ben doesn't respond I get nervous that I have said the wrong thing and insulted him.

"Was that ok to say?"

"My love, you can say anything. In fact, I have a deeply, sincere request that you do. Tell me anything you feel in your heart, mind, and body... at the very moment you experience it. I want to know everything, in real time. Tell me what you need, what you feel, or even if you just don't know. Let's make it a practice, in and out of bed."

Oh my gosh, the thought of saying every thought and feeling in bed makes me blush. This is a very new concept for me. I feel tongue-tied already.

But Ben continues, "I'm asking as a favor to me. It's what I want. I want to be fully aware of you. It will help me so much if you tell me as it is happening. I want your heart to be transparent to me. And when I feel something, I promise I'll express it to you, the best I can. I know we are human and it's natural that we'll be scared to say things, to protect our egos, and things will come out the wrong way, but it's so much better to try. That way there aren't all these lingering questions or doubts. We can just say. It will make our relationship so much deeper and more pleasurable. Communication is key. Ginny, I love you. I don't want any doubts that may lead to insecurities. You have no reason to be insecure as far as my heart and desire for you is concerned. I am all yours and in truth, I want you all for myself."

And with those words, my whole being relaxes into his arms, for that is precisely what I desire.

Chapter Thirty-Seven

As amazing as my days with Ben are, I know it is time to see Fredrick again. I can't hide from him and the situation forever, although the thought of doing so sounds wonderful and is incredibly tempting. How will Fredrick respond to me? It seems that the way people respond in these kinds of situations can be very telling about their personalities and about the future of the relationship. I sheepishly make my way towards Fredrick's apartment. I feel like I've shrunk three inches. When I arrive, I knock, even though I have a key. It's just that now I feel even more like a guest, a stranger if not an enemy. But the truth is that I always felt like an outsider in this place.

When Fredrick opens the door, I feel myself shiver as if a cold wind just blew over me. These past weeks I've gotten so used to Ben's decidedly sunny disposition that in contrast, just walking into the dark apartment and seeing Fredrick's gloomy figure and somber countenance all seems so desolate, devoid of love and warmth.

His stare is harsh, "Hello. Have a seat," he says coldly.

I realize as I sit on the couch, made to feel like a scolded school-girl at the principal's office, all of my past expectations for our life together, the few that remained, have just died. How could

I be so blind? His stare is icy and his tone is funeral. Every ending is a beginning as well, I have new ambitions and new goals for a different kind of love, one where I feel truly loved for me, the good, the bad, and the ugly.

"Ginny, your mind is not as subtle as I once thought," he is speaking in a barely audible whisper that still sounds mostly like a roar. "Your actions, and your recent inactions; I had no idea that you could be both so wild and disappointing," he looks through me, his vision blind to me, "like some impetuous child."

His words crash down across my back, like a lash, and the abusive chess match begins anew.

Fredrick looks bitterly across the room. I stand my ground.

"I believe we both were doing the best we could," I am trying to reign in the burning anger of the moment.

Fredrick cackles in a way that sends shivers up my spine, "That's all you have to offer?"

I summon up my courage and continue, "You were blind to me."

"I flew you here; I proposed marriage to you; I dined you; I shared my home and my work with you. You call *that* blind?"

"You were indifferent to me from the moment I arrived here. I have never felt so alone as I have here and in your company."

"I am so tired of your feelings, Ginny. I gave you all I had in me, all that I could. You should be so lucky as to have a partner like me to collaborate with. Your ideas are childish, your dissertation riddled with inaccuracies. I did not choose you for your feelings, I chose you because I thought you were smarter and more well-spoken than most women." He speaks with a tone of utter dismissal and disdain and then for a wavering second I see it, the hardness turns soft and his lips begin to tremble. I think he is about to cry. But instead he says, turning away, "Fine then. If that's how you feel, I wash my hands of you."

As he looks down at his feet, I remember the little boy he spoke of, and some of my fears and drives towards my own new hopes and dreams recede into the background. I feel a slight stirring of tenderness towards him. In front of me is an acutely unhappy man, a man who has not chosen his lot in life as much as it has chosen him. And given his personality and way of being in the world, I wonder if he will ever find happiness, with or without me. There was a glimmer of light in him when he wrote that letter I read on the plane to Geneva, but he has gone back to the gloom of his steadfast, Cimmerian work ethic. It's not that work is bad, on the contrary, I know as well as anybody that it can save a life, but it cannot, *alone*, in and of itself, *make* a life. Ben has so clearly pointed that out to me of late, for which I am very grateful. We all need work, some more than others, and I do need it, Ben does too, but for Fredrick it always did and always will come first, and *that* a relationship cannot weather. I cannot weather that, maybe someone else can. I hope for Fredrick's sake that he finds the person who will. Or maybe it's the life he wants, a life without deep love, one seemingly without much love at all. That seems to be the path for some people, but it is not the one for me. This I am learning all too well. Thank goodness. Ben! Just thinking of Ben sheds light and warmth into my soul. So much so, that I just want to wish Fredrick well and shed a sliver of light into his life, but once again, he lets his acrimony brood and blow, and it flows lava-like over us. His indignation covers us in its ashes.

I decide to take responsibility for my part in this mess. In large part because I will feel better if this situation is somehow smoothed out. I know myself well enough to know that it will be harder for me to live in the world if I don't.

"I'm sorry for speaking as I did and for running out of the restaurant. And for my long silent absence since. I really wasn't sure what to do, and I'm afraid I did not act correctly or well."

"I agree and I'm glad you acknowledge the immaturity and unsociability of your behavior. I've never seen such a display."

It was such a characteristic and predictable response. He is in no way going to make this easy on me. Why do people have to be so themselves?

I feel shaken by his demeanor and wonder what I would do if Ben was not here for me, literally waiting for me in the café around the corner. If I didn't know that I will soon go and tell Ben everything, that he will sit and listen to everything I have to relate and have so much understanding and insight, and that he will hold my hand as I do, and afterward hold me tight, kiss my cheek, and in these ways help make everything alright, who knows what I would do were that not the case? All of a sudden I feel incredibly grateful for the freedom of choice and strength that having Ben in my life gives me at this moment.

There is silence. Fredrick sits there looking condemning. I don't know what to do next.

"Do you think we should talk about it?" My heart is pounding more in fear of his response than anything else. Fredrick is very angry, and the dour expression on his face makes him look all the less attractive to me. His look is in such contrast to the sunny smile I have grown accustomed to. Ben exudes light. It was fitting that I first noticed him playing with the particles in a sun ray. I cannot help but believe that Ben would be kind in such a moment of penitence. I could be wrong, but I don't believe Ben could muster this anger and coldness. I feel a tear fall. Oh no, here it comes.

"There is not much to talk about Virginia. You have created a very unwanted, undeserved, and much disliked mental disturbance in my life such that I've been distracted from my work. I don't appreciate the distraction and don't wish for any more agitation."

What? Is this his pride talking? Can he not access any other emotions? My goodness, everything he is saying serves to cement my decision *not* to be with him.

"Aren't you even going to ask where I've been?"

"I think I'm smart enough to know that one. And I am thoroughly unimpressed."

It's as if he is too proud to speak of his jealousy, and yet he is jealous to the bone. I can feel that. But it's a jealousy stemming from ego, not passion. Yikes. His ego takes up the whole room. There is no room for anything or anyone else; no place for me. If only he could show some tenderness, some caring, we would still be over but at least I could think of him more fondly. His way of being will only serve to drive me further into Ben's arms. In some ways I know that although it doesn't feel like it right now, this response of Fredrick's makes my decision and actions easier to bear.

Then my own ire suddenly rears its head. Bring it Fredrick, this is what you've got? This is what you're made of? I am just glad I did not marry you. Fredrick breaks my internalized train of thought by speaking,

"So are you back now? Should we go get some lunch?"

I am totally taken aback. It takes me a moment to get my bearings and answer him.

"No. No thank you. I truly am sorry how things have turned out, but I am not feeling like eating or very much like talking anymore." While it is not a forthright 'fuck you,' I am proud of myself for speaking these words. It is my nature to continue a conversation when others want to, but I foresee future interactions with Fredrick to be very draining, certainly no fun, highly uncomfortable, and ultimately not good for me. So why continue?

I grab my bag from the couch and stand up to leave. It feels like a very long way from the couch to the door. I see the front door beckoning at the end of the small corridor as if it is my salvation. I just need to walk through it and find Ben. I turn to look at Fredrick. He seems confused and angry more than hurt.

"Fine. Congratulations Ginny, your thesis is worthless. And so is Ben."

More than his words, it is the look in his eye that disturbs me. There is malice and ill content. What does he mean by that? I need to get out of here.

"Good bye, Fredrick."

I walk out. As soon as the door closes behind me and I am on the other side of it, I feel freer. I breathe again. My heart felt so leaden in that apartment. Now as I make my way out of the building, it's as if someone has removed a concrete block from my chest. I walk at a very quickened pace out of the building to the café.

Chapter Thirty-Eight

Just seeing Ben's back makes my heart leap. There is something about the precise width of his shoulders that makes me feel safe again. When he turns around and I see the concerned and caring look in his eyes, I know it will be okay. I take a deep breath and go to his table and take my place in the chair opposite him. It is my spot, where I belong. He leans in across the table, and clasps my hands in his.

"Someone needs to make these tables smaller," he says.

So many times the expanse of the table between us has seemed too vast. Before Ben, I had never noticed that.

Keeping my hands in his, his expression looks more anxious than I have ever witnessed upon his countenance. I don't like being the cause of that, but I am anxious too. Fredrick's words loom heavily.

"So...how did it go? Wait just a sec before you tell me..." He leans over and places a tender kiss on my lips. It's the best gift he could give me.

"I did it," my voice waivers, my brow furrows.

Ben looks confused and worried.

"Well, he's *so* weird. He was so angry and cold, and almost threatening. I don't get it. Anyway, the point is I left. It's done."

As I say those words, my stomach turns. I do wonder what Fredrick meant.

I see Ben looks agitated and I want to reassure him, "Anyway, whatever he is thinking, the truth is I am completely clear in my heart and head. It's over, and I want to be with you so much, it's ridiculous."

Ben smiles. "Let's get out of here." As we stand, he pulls me closer, his arm around my waist. I love to be in his arms.

***

We walk and talk all the way back to Ben's place, quite a ways, hand in hand. He seems to intuitively know that I need the concrete distance, both in miles and time, between what happened at Fredrick's apartment and now.

Once home, Ben pours me a glass of wine and puts on some jazz. He knows just how to relax me.

"Here," he says, handing me a glass of pinot grigio. Lay here and I'm going to give you a massage. After today, you could use one."

He kisses me gently and lifts my dress above my head. I lay on my stomach on the bed, face down, and soon recognize the smell of lavender. The scent alone soothes me. Then, I feel the drips of lavender oil slowly and sensually drizzled upon my back. Ben's knees straddle my outer thighs and I close my eyes. Ben's hands are strong and their movements on my shoulder and neck allow me to release from all the tension that came before. He spends all the time in the world on my neck and shoulders making sure there is no spot that feels unloved. He makes his way down my back. I am aware of both of his hands on my upper arms and shoulders, massaging them tenderly but firmly, and then I feel something else. He has without using his hands, gently entered me. Oh my. In addition to his hands on me, rubbing lovingly, I feel his hard cock massaging me from the inside. It's almost too much pleasure. I hear my own gratefully toned moan reflected back to me, though I am not aware of making the sounds.

"Feel good?" I hear him ask, bringing me back somewhat with his voice.

"It feels amazing," I get the words out, although I am on the verge of coming. I arch my back in pleasure, also knowing that at the same time it gives him a view he'll enjoy and a different angle. He thrusts into me, and I love the strength of it. He reaches a part of me no one ever has. And then he slows down, as he is in me, I feel his thumb, I think, gently exploring my behind, and it's as if I know what he is thinking. I feel the drips of more oil on my buttocks, being massaged in. I have never done this, never dreamed of it, never thought I would. But now I know I will. I feel I will do anything with and for this man. He is my partner. I feel the oil on and in me, as he massages my ass. I feel my backside rise in the air to him. And then, I feel him, where I never thought another would be, and he fills me up. I hear him moan so deeply. I breathe around him, letting him into me, deeper and deeper. I feel a very sensual pain. I don't want it to end, but I also don't know how long I can go. Just at the right moment, I feel him come inside me as he calls out to the heavens. He almost collapses onto my slippery back. He lays there. We lay there, our hands entwined in each others'. I feel we have transcended my own boundaries, like a country being taken over by a beneficent ruler, but I also know that I have welcomed him. I think to myself, I never want this take over to end. It's been quite the coup.

Chapter Thirty-Nine

I lay on the blanket on the grass, in the late-morning sun, by the lake, beside Ben. As we both read, I keep looking up at Ben and my thoughts turn to our love making last night. It went places I never thought I'd visit, and I can hardly concentrate on anything else. I seem to be on a "books about Daisy" kick; *The Great Gatsby*, which is one of Ben's favorites and which I grabbed off his shelf before our walk, while certainly catchy, pales in comparison to what happened in our bed last night.

"What are you thinking about?" he asks, with a cat that ate the canary grin.

"Oh nothing," I blush, "well, what do you think?"

He laughs and puts his book down, and leans over to kiss me.

"I think it was wonderful, thank you, baby."

"You're most welcome, my love," and we just look into each other's eyes. I think to myself that we are that gorgeously in love couple I watched yearningly at the restaurant, the one where the man kissed the crumb from the corner of the woman's lip, the one I longed to be like. That is us, and more.

***

Following a slow, restful day of a walk, picnic, reading, and a nap under a tree, Ben takes my hand and leads me home. I'm pretty sure my outgoing email message, if it were honest, would say: "Out of office message: Unbelievably happy and mostly in bed."

After last night, I have been looking forward to making love all day. Ben has, rather unusually, made me wait for it. And still is. He seems a little distracted tonight, and our dinner, while delicious, seems to take a long time. As we sip our wine, I ask him expectantly, "Are you done? I'll clear the plates if you are."

He laughs, "Is there somewhere you need to be?"

"Well, as a matter of fact, yes," and I can't believe I'm saying this and being so forward. "I need to be in bed with you."

He pauses for a quick second with a sad and lost stare, then seems to snap out of it, shifting abruptly.

"You certainly don't need to tell me twice," he says and picks me up and carries me to the bed. He starts to take off my clothes, slowly and assuredly. Watching me intensely with each body part exposed. First my shirt, as he gazes at me in my bra—another La Perla purchase. He looks so pleased.

"It's very lovely, but this is going away now," he says and throws it to the floor. He cups my breasts in his hands and I see the pleasure he gets from holding them. He takes one in his mouth and cradles my nipple in his lips, playfully and then harder as he plays with the other with his fingers. I am enraptured by his delighted attention of sucking my breasts.

Eventually, he moves to my suede skirt and takes it off. He looks at me, naked but for my thong (another recent acquisition from my new favorite store). He smiles gorgeously.

"You are so sexy."

He pushes my panties to the side and plays with me, his hands going in and out of and all around my slit. He moans when he feels how wet I am and throws his head back as he feels around.

"You slay me," he tells me.

Then he removes the thong and looks at me naked, on my back, on the bed. I don't dare move. Ben gently but quite firmly pushes my thighs apart, so that they are spread wider than I knew they could go. He just gazes at me and I feel vulnerable, exposed. But I want to be. I want him to have all of me. I remind myself to breathe and relax, let the energy move downwards and then circle through. His hands on my outer thighs, it feels like he gazes down at me forever, completely enraptured by my anatomy, and then he decides to explore me inside and out. He is at once both strong and winsome. I feel the strength of his hands and know that I will soon feel the strength of his cock. But I also sense his wonderment as I allow him to experience me, as a woman fully. For a moment I am reminded of seeing him play with the particles in the light at the cathedral, and I feel like he plays with my clitoris and my ass with a similar wonderment. I want him to play all he wants; I let him. He is enchanted. His pleasure noises tell me so. When he has tasted and licked and sucked and felt all around me, inside and out, and made me come so hard, he stands by the bed, lifts my body just to the edge of the bed, spreads my legs even further, his hands holding my calves, and enters me. It is all I want in the world.

He moves gently in and out as he looks me deeply in the eyes.

"Oh my sweet, I'm coming," he moans.

As he does, I hold him close and wrap my legs and arms around him. He is completely in my embrace. I am his home. I love that he tells me when he is coming and I love that I can hold him knowing he is. He is so right—communication is key. We stay looking into each other's eyes, so naturally now. I am no longer shy like I was.

"Thank you" I tell him. "I love you." I gently kiss his brow. I feel completely content.

Chapter Forty

The real world intrudes; Ben slept restlessly and woke up abruptly. He said he had some errands to run today, so I decide to take some time for myself. It's been a while, and it feels good to walk around the city alone. I visit some shops I haven't seen. It is so unlike me to do this. Jacqui would be thrilled. Then I decide to take in some art at the modern galleries in the very hip section of town, Quartier des Bains. Ben would be proud. With every painting and sculpture I see that moves me in some way, I think of how I'll describe it to Ben later tonight over dinner. I imagine us sipping wine and me telling him about my day, and him telling me about his. My soul warms at the thought. Then thinking of the love we'll likely make tonight, oh my....I get distracted. I wonder if anyone passing by can tell what I'm thinking. I'm pretty sure I just blushed.

***

Having spent the entire day in ways that are quite unusual for me, I make my way back to our apartment. The day got away from me at the galleries, and I haven't spoken with Ben since he left this morning. He is the only person that I know who doesn't have a cell phone. While it is frustrating at times, I also respect his belief that the convenience is not worth the potential damage that phones can do to both a relationship and one's peace of mind. I'd always harbored that suspicion of technology myself, and it's been a relief to be with someone who isn't always on their phone. I know things aren't all sorted out, but I'm starting to believe they will be soon. As I approach, I notice an envelope taped to the front door with my name on it. I laugh to myself because my immediate thought is, "Oh another plane ticket, perhaps another proposal," but I don't think life repeats quite so completely and symmetrically and I'm pretty sure Ben would not follow Fredrick's lead in any direction, ever. I open it:

Dearest Ginny,

This is an insanely difficult letter to write. This is the hardest decision I have ever had to make, and while I know that you won't understand why I have to go, trust that I love you. By the time you read this, I will be on a plane to DC. Very suddenly and unexpectedly, there is an opening for an assistant professor in political science at Georgetown University. You need to finish your thesis and I need to go out on my own and see if this position is one I will be good at. Work is important. I know if anyone can understand this, it's you. I need to make something of my life and get out of the way of your success. I'm so sorry to leave like this, Ginny. One day you will understand.

Love,

Ben

What? This doesn't make any sense at all. Ben leaving, without saying goodbye, and for *work*! Of all things for work? Are you fucking kidding me? This must be a joke. And why didn't he ask me to come with him?

I turn the key in the lock quickly and partly expect Ben to be there with flowers in the middle of the room, throwing some wacky surprise party for me or something. But seeing as we hardly know anyone here, this also seems unlikely.

As I enter the apartment, I can immediately tell that Ben is not here, that his few possessions are gone and he has vacated this space and in turn my life. My body turns hot with anger, then cold with fear. As if I have just turned to marble, the life flows out of me. The feeling of lost hope and abandonment pervades my soul and makes me sadder than I've felt in a very, very long time. I collapse onto the couch. This cannot be my life.

Chapter Forty-One

For a long time, I just sit, dumbstruck, numb, fallen. Then I get up to walk, around the apartment, zombie sleuth like, looking for clues. There is not a trace of him save for the distant scent of his body on the sheets of the bed. I feel like I must leave and go outside or I will wither up into nothing.

I feel so completely ill at ease; feelings of separation haunt every cell in my body. As I walk, so many questions and scenarios run through my head. Once again I am struck by the fact that I hardly know anyone here, except for two people. And one has left the country. I'll look for Fredrick. Maybe he can fill in some of the blanks for me.

***

I find Fredrick in the library, and for once he immediately steps outside with me, seeing on my face that I mean business.

"What is going on, Fredrick?"

"You mean about Ben leaving, I presume"

"Yes, I do." So he knows.

"Well, Ben seemed to believe you would think the better of him for it."

"Did you want him to take the position?"

"I don't really care one way or the other what he does."

"I would have thought that you would care somewhat about his welfare. He was your assistant for four years."

"I would have been better off without him, obviously. And so would and will you. If you really want to know, since you are asking, I personally think the reason he took the position is because of a certain Leila Court, whom I believe Ben has been seeing for years. He's a player, that boy of yours. It's what he does. He looks innocent and sweet, but he is a lover of women and pleasure, a man-whore with no intention to inhabit the real world. He seduces women and then let's them down. I thought you were smart and practical enough to see that for yourself. It doesn't surprise me at all that he made a mess of everything and then ran off. You always say it yourself—what's your line, 'people are themselves,' know your customers. I always suspected he was ultimately a good for nothing gypsy who would make nothing of himself. But maybe, if he doesn't fuck it up, with this academic position, he'll actually prove me wrong. I doubt it. But one way or the other, I don't think you and I need to speak any more about him. He is finally out of our lives."

Just then I am so enraged and confused that I decide it is not worth speaking any more to Fredrick about this, or anything at all, ever again.

***

Myriad emotions have flowed through me in the last twenty-four hours, but at this moment, my insecurity about being played for a fool is the strongest thing I can feel. It is overwhelming. I feel hurt and confused and left. I feel lonely and most acutely, unloved. How could I have been so painstakingly mistaken? Did Ben just use me these past weeks, so he could get his sexual pleasure, make his conquest, and then move on to the woman he was with before, maybe even with all along? I opened up to Ben and then got thrown under the bus. All I can bear to do is curl up in a ball and hope the pain dissipates during sleep. I pray for some respite in dreamland.

***

I awake with a jolt as the cruel thought of my situation hits me and I jump start from sleep as if coming out of a nightmare. I'm a fool. The only man I've ever loved is gone. He was my only real lover and my greatest friend. I feel overcome by the dissonance in my mind and heart. Why did I let myself love him so fully and deeply? And all so quickly? Was his kindness all just some great game and conquest for him, just to prove to himself that he could get me to love him? This troubling thought irks and haunts me so. I am on my knees in the bathroom. Tears pour like rain. I decide I can't stay here. It's time to leave. I want nothing more to do with Geneva. It has given and taken away too much.

Chapter Forty-Two

Washington, DC is like a stranger to me. For days and days, I hardly leave the little rental apartment I found. The sky is sunny but I am a limp rag. The fever of my love has turned into a full blown flu. I have spent my entire life trying to avoid feelings just like this; I am ill equipped. I can't take this. It has been days and days since I have locked myself away from the world, basking in the shades-drawn, never-ending darkness.

At some point, there is a knock on the door. It is Jacqui.

"Please, Gigi. Can I come in?"

"What are you doing here?"

"You aren't answering your phone. It's what sisters do. Let me in. Now."

I open the door. Jacqui stares at my ghostly frame.

"Oh Gigi," she wraps her arms around me. "I'm so sorry. You are so thin. If I'd known it was this way, I would have come even earlier."

Jacqui is the other great love of my life, so my heart begins to settle a little.

For a long time Jacqui just holds me in a warm hug as I curl up in her arms like a child. While I came to DC, of all places, specifically because Jacqui and Evan had temporarily relocated here for Evan's work, I had not really reached out to her—not wanting to burden her with my immense sadness.

"First love, eh?" Jacqui touches my cheek.

"Yeah, it's brutal. I am definitely not cut out for this shit."

"It gets easier," she says.

"When?"

"With time."

"I guess so," I murmur; I know she is rationally correct but it doesn't feel, in this moment, like time will heal me.

I take a deep breath. I feel hollow.

"The first step is leaving the apartment and eating," she grabs me by the arm and pulls me into the sunlight.

***

At the restaurant, I choke down a few sips of soup. The thought of chewing something is sickening to me. I cannot bear anything pleasurable, food, music, touch, they all remind me of Ben. We so thoroughly explored all of the range of our senses. That was his thing. That was the whole meaning of tantra, the divine exploration of the senses. I feel strip-mined, empty, and there are no words within me to explain this to Jacqui. In fact, I can't talk, so instead I sit quietly and slurp my soup. I feel pathetic but I can do no other.

I hear Jacqui saying as if from afar, "I want to find something for you to do that will make you feel good. Some volunteer job that will ensure that you leave the house, so you will feel connected to the world, useful and needed."

It's funny to hear her talking this way. She used to give me such a hard time about all of my volunteer work. She used to call it my boyfriend. She would tell me all of my 'do-gooder work' was just a way of avoiding life and relationships, and now here we have come full circle.

Tears brim along the edges of my eyes about to pour over, completely unconvincingly I respond, "Sure, that sounds good."

I hastily get up from the table and step out into the street. I don't want to cry at a restaurant, and yet these emotions are inescapable. Ben owns me and all of my pleasure, all of my touch, my sounds, my taste, my feel, my sight. That's what we did; we handed it all over to each other. Everywhere I look, he is there, his delicate kisses, his fire-blue eyes, his breath, his smooth, sonorous voice, his supple skin, the taste of his lips. I miss all of him. We return to the apartment and I fall back into bed, Jacqui beside me, and I cry myself to sleep.

***

Does he miss me? I wake up with this thought and a belly full of loathing, ruing that this love affair ever began. The sadness lulls me to sleep at night and the fear awakens me. Today is the day I am actually supposed to show up somewhere, at the teaching hospital. Jacqui arranged it. She signed me up to be a volunteer at the surgical center. I'll be helping elderly people navigate the pre-surgical paperwork and process, to help soothe their nerves and ease their anxiety.

I manage to shower and comb my hair. I braid it. I have so few clothes here in DC and I haven't had the energy to do laundry, so the only clean thing I have to wear is the pink dress I wore the night Ben and I met at the park, the first night we made love. It seems such an unnecessary and cruel detail. I pull the dress over my head. It drapes across my gaunt frame. I look in the mirror. It doesn't look quite like it used to look. I am a ghostly version of myself, but I have no choice. This is the only thing I have to wear today. I should have thought this through. If there were not so many broken pieces of me, I could have.

***

Nervously, I walk through the hospital doors. There is a woman at the reception desk looking attentively my direction. Near me, another woman in a wheelchair holds a scared child in her lap. I notice two elderly couples are huddled together with clipboards. These are much worse circumstances than mine. I take a deep breath. With each glance and breath I gain a bit more perspective; I step forward to the desk.

"May I help you?" the overtly bored but courteous woman asks.

"I am here to register as a volunteer."

"Great. The volunteer coordinator's office is on the third floor. Take the G elevator to room 3947," she hands me a map. I already feel as though some purpose has come back into my life. Jacqui knows me. I need altruistic work. It is who I am. It is my best medicine; it heals me.

Chapter Forty-Three

For the first time since everything went down (and out), I went to sleep without the fits and starts. My monkey mind was somewhat soothed and lulled by a very full day's work of tending to others in substantial need.

But I still woke up angry. Sometimes I wake up sad, sometimes a somnambulist who has forgotten in the night all that has happened only to be jarred into reality as I remember the situation. I alternate between caring, loving feelings toward Ben that are peppered with sorrow in the face of his betrayal of me, and the ones I feel today. Today I woke up scornful. And you know, there is actually something appealing to the energy that my anger awakens. I want to be distracted, as distracted from my feelings as possible. I want to help others and be in the world, out of my head and heart—caring less than I do. The anger, much more than the sorrow, seems to fuel this desire to get up and go and to let go.

This morning, Jacqui notices the spring in my step. "There is something alive in your eyes. Has something happened, Gigi?"

"Too much has happened. I just want to move on."

I see that Jacqui is unconvinced and worried about me but I go stridently about my day, helping at the hospital like it is the air

I breathe. Each person I see I ask what I can do for them. It is a manic altruism. I keep myself as busy as possible, opening my heart in different directions, towards others. For the moment, this is keeping my troubles at bay.

And I write. Whenever I have a spare hour or even half an hour, I pull out my laptop and get to work. I take out the copy of my dissertation that Ben had read. He had left it in a drawer in our Geneva apartment. It was the only physical thing I took with me that would remind me of him. Still everything reminds me of him. His marginalia, his comments in the margins, are insightful. I address each one, page by page, day by day. It's coming along. This is one thing I have control over. In the moments that my head clears and my heart allows, I write. My dissertation will be done soon.

***

By the end of days like this, I am, thankfully, exhausted. Partly from the work, partly from trying so hard not to feel the pain. As I sit on my bed, it all topples down. The energy that comes with acrimony dissipates and the hurt comes through even stronger than before. I cry into my hands. I do love Ben, so deeply. I thought he was the one for me. I saw my life ahead of me, a life I had never pictured or envisioned before. The saddest thing now, what haunts me the most, is that the seeds we planted together will never grow into the garden that tantalized me, that I fervently believed, somewhere in my heart, would bloom, even if my head warned me otherwise. I miss him terribly. I miss what could have been and what I thought, in spite of myself and my own warnings to myself, would one day be.

***

Jacqui meets me for lunch; I think she is trying to get some food into me, bless her. As she eats and I play with the food on my plate, moving the Thai noodles this way then that, she is speaking about "all the other fish in the sea."

"Gigi, there is the right guy out there for you. Someone much much sexier and kinder than Fredrick. Which isn't hard to imagine."

I let her digs at Fredrick slide. I have neither the will nor the energy to defend him.

"And someone much more grounded and reliable than Ben. Also not hard to imagine. Someone you can count on; someone sexy and loving, but who's got his act together and won't let you down, who will really show up for you. And then will continue to show up."

I hear her words, but I can truly think of no one but Ben. I know she is thinking of her Evan. And I am glad she has found someone who fits her so well.

Jacqui says I can do much better than Ben. One thing about me is that when I truly care about someone, I will not keep silent if they are insulted. Even if they have hurt me and I am so angry with them.

"Please, Jacqui," my lips tremble, "Don't speak ill of him. My heart just can't take it. The world feels ugly enough without such talk."

***

I am not one to sit in my own calamitous thoughts for too long. So every day I pour myself into my work, I volunteer and I write. And I walk. I walk DC, from place to place, averaging eight miles a day, some days more. I will wear out my muscles so that my mind and heart may possibly rest. And I will speak with others, spread out my feelings for others, dissipate the love that was so directed towards Ben.

I begin to feel a modicum of well-being now that I can somewhat return to my focus on improving others' lots, by finishing the body of work that I started, and by exhausting my body physically through exercise. Geneva was not good for me. My mind was too much on myself; it was corrosive. But here, there is so much good for me to do that my own heart-pangs will be distracted. Just waking up knowing I will make a difference to someone today is so much better than waking up wondering if someone will take notice of and be gentle with and loving towards me. What a petty fool I was there. I lost sight of what makes me happy.

Chapter Forty-Four

Today at the hospital, I am early and should eat. I should really eat more in general, even without Jacqui to prod and encourage me to do so. I've been sleeping a bit better, and exercising, but the food...I need to take in nourishment. My self-starvation, as unconscious and unwanted as it has been, is so very symptomatic. I need to nourish myself, not wait for love to feed me. I feel like I lost myself with Fredrick. I was so impressed with his accomplishments and ego that I allowed myself to become invisible. But I also lost myself with Ben. He became an addiction, and I forgot my work and who I am. I gave over my power to both of them. I don't want to ever do that again.

Last week, I finished my thesis and finally submitted it to the department. It felt good to do the work, the culmination of four years of study and writing. Professor Patel was most pleased. And although I cannot imagine a next time, if there is a next time, I must remember to hold onto myself and my work while being in love. My mother once told me, "Don't fall in love, stand in love."

I rise up from my desk and ask a co-worker, "Where is the cafeteria?" because I've never been there, and now I have some time.

"It's here on the main floor. Follow the hallway to the right. There will be signs."

I thank her and walk down the hall.

As I approach the cafeteria, my stomach aches and my skin begins to prickle. My anxiety is building. Has my anxiety really gotten this bad? I ponder. I take a few deep breaths and continue down the corridor. My heart is racing. This is ridiculous, I think to myself. I am feeling faint. I round the bend of the hallway determined to push through this emotional state. There is no basis, I say aloud to myself. My eyes to the ground, I make the last turn to the cafeteria. I'm sure some food will settle my nerves. I haven't been eating enough; it makes me jittery and even more shaky than I already am from nerves.

I grab a tray and some yogurt and coffee. I check my watch. There is still enough time. The line is long and my legs are now tingling too. What is going on with me? I step up to the cashier and position my tray.

"$5.49," she looks at me with a dull indifference.

"Thanks."

I smile as I step forward once again with my tray, he catches my eye. Ben is in a full embrace with another woman. He is holding her and tenderly caressing her hair. This cannot be. How can this be? Yet I am watching it. She is lovely, so, so pretty. My whole being scrunches in on itself, and I immediately feel utterly sick to my stomach. What? How and why are they here?

The tray slips from my fingers to the ground. There is a loud crash. Everyone stares. Ben looks up at me. His mouth gapes open. Tears are streaming from my eyes. I decide to leave the tray on the ground and run as quickly as I can back down the long corridor of the hospital. I want out. Fredrick had warned me, yet somehow, I didn't believe that it could be true. My hands turn as cold as blocks of ice.

Chapter Forty-Five

"Ginny, Ginny," I hear my name and refuse to believe this person could be calling out for me. I keep going, eyes straight ahead. Get me out of here.

"Please, wait, Ginny!" the woman's voice calls out again.

I stop and pause as the petite woman with curly blonde hair whose hand Ben was holding, runs up to me.

"Wait, Ginny...."

Against my better judgment, I stop. What the hell is going on? I'm in a surreal dream, and I must wake soon.

"Ginny, hi," she looks at me with a stirring tenderness that takes me aback. I do not understand her solicitous expression. She seems stopped in time, herself breathing deeply and steadily as if to calm me via her own breathing pattern.

"I'm Leila. I'm Ben's sister. Please, please, give me a moment and let me explain..."

Ben's sister? What?

"We're here, Ben and I, with our aunt, at the hospital. She's very ill. Ben couldn't believe it was you just now. He froze and panicked so I ran after you. Ginny, I've been with Ben since he left Geneva and took the Georgetown University position. I know the whole story. Ben keeps retelling it to me. It is tearing him up inside—he is positively sick about it. Trust me, he has been a total wreck. I've never seen him like this, not even close. He thinks for sure that you would never want to speak to him again after he left like he did. But he has told me so much about you, and I know in my heart that if you have it in you to just hear me out, then you will understand."

I am stunned. I can't believe this is happening. I can't believe that this is my life. But Leila is so gentle. She takes my hand so caringly. It's as if I am familiar with that touch. I am frozen like a statue, but I am starting to thaw by the ray of warmth emanating from Leila Court.

"Ginny, can we please go for coffee or better yet a glass of wine? I'll tell you what happened. You need to know.....I always thought you deserved to know."

Her demeanor disarms me. Tearily, I let her guide me, her hand on my arm, out of the hospital and to a restaurant next door.

Chapter Forty-Six

Leila leads me to a quiet table tucked away in the corner. Red or white she asks? I ask her to choose; I cannot think. She orders a bottle of red.

"This might take a while," she begins, and I listen intently and in disbelief to every word.

"Ok, I'm just going to tell you what Ben has told me. From what I understand, the day before Ben left Geneva, Fredrick had emailed him and told him they needed to meet immediately. The next day, Fredrick told Ben that a political science professor, a colleague at Georgetown University, had received a dreadful health diagnosis and there was an opening, *immediately* for the position. It needed to be filled *toute de suite* as the students were in mid-semester and Fredrick had recommended Ben to the department and told them Ben could fill in the classes pronto— like the very next day. That, of course, is unusual, was Fredrick's selling point, and they said ok. Fredrick told Ben to take the opening and to be on the plane later that evening. Fredrick had set it all up; he even bought Ben a plane ticket. Ben must leave immediately and begin teaching this man's courses. And in turn, later in the semester, when the department would do the real search, Ben would be in line to take over the position full-time. Fredrick himself would make sure of it."

I'm listening but it doesn't add up. "So what? That's so stupid. Ben chose a job over me? And didn't even talk it over with me? I would have encouraged him to take it. Heck, I would have gone with him!"

"Of course, you would have… that makes perfect sense. And that's precisely what Ben thought. He told Fredrick that he couldn't leave you, and that he had to talk with you first. That things needed to slow down just a bit. And yes, he wanted to take you with him if he took it and if you would go with him. Of course he did, he loves you so much, Ginny."

"Bullshit. I'm sorry, but that I don't believe. Look what he did."

"Ginny, Fredrick told Ben this was his chance to actually make something of himself. That it had fallen into his lap, in spite of his 'loose and pathetic' ways. Fredrick told Ben that you, Ginny, needed a man with a future, who would do well for himself and for you. Fredrick weaved a tale about how it was why you were drawn to him."

"Fredrick was wrong. Yes, maybe it was for his erudition but not his ambition."

"Regardless, Fredrick did succeed in tapping into Ben's deep-seated insecurities. Ben told me how important work is to you, Ginny. And Fredrick reminded Ben of the chasm between the two of you—how you have real intellectual ideas and the potential to be an academic superstar, *if* you were not stymied, distracted, and ultimately held back by the likes of Ben."

"That's horrible." I can't bear to hear it, but I know I must. I am so thankful that Leila pours more wine, and that she ordered the bottle.

"But Ben should have known better. He knows me. I am not like that. I cared so much for and about him."

"He knows and feels the same. He told Fredrick to shove it, that he was bringing you with him or not taking the position, that no job was worth losing you over. Then Fredrick dropped a bomb on him. He told Ben that while you and Ben had been off together, Fredrick had boiled down, summarized, and basically outright stolen some of your dissertation conclusions. He wrote them up in an article that has been accepted by a big journal in your field. He told Ben that if he publishes it, your work becomes plagiarism and obsolete overnight. He out and out blackmailed Ben to leave immediately, without so much as speaking to you, and *only by doing that*, would Fredrick *withhold* from publishing the article. Fredrick outright threatened Ben with destroying your work if he made any contact with you ever again. If Fredrick found out Ben contacted you, he'd give the editors of the publication the go ahead. Ben has told me this story over and over again, it's how Fredrick got back at him for stealing your heart. Fredrick is such a bad guy. Sorry to say, but it's true. He planned on further ruining Ben's reputation, if he didn't leave immediately, by making it known that his research assistant had an affair with his fiance. Ben knew Fredrick is too proud to put such a blow to his own ego out there in the world, so Ben was not worried about that particular threat. And Ben doesn't care about those things. But Ben *was* terribly worried and devastated about you losing all your hard work. He left to protect you, Ginny. That's what he thought. Honestly, Ginny, I told him it sounded like a bad move. But he did do it to save your work and career. He really felt that ultimately, that was what was most important."

I feel sick to my stomach. I don't know what to think or do.

Chapter Forty-Seven

Upon hearing the details of the insane conditions of Ben's sudden and disastrous departure, I feel myself go numb. All of a sudden everything seems to change. Like a huge, sudden shift in the weather, but instead of the climate, it's quite possibly my whole life. So abruptly, the dream of being with Ben, really being with him, as balanced partners in life, feels like a possibility again. I am startled out of my reverie as I hear Leila say, "Ben also thought that perhaps by taking the professor position, he could fill the gap between you. And that maybe one day you could be together. He never wanted you to be moving down by being with him."

I'm confused, "Moving down, how?"

Leila looks pained in explaining, her lips curve downwards, "Down some social ladder, or something, even though that's something I know Ben doesn't care about. You know he could care less about fortune and prestige for their own sakes. But he cares very much about anything that could separate you two. And he believes that you truly deserve a very good if not grand life— even if you'd never say so. He didn't want to drag you down by being with him, in any way shape or form. Ben worships you Ginny—he did in Geneva, he does so now in his heart. Trust me, he wants to live the love you have for each other out in the moment. That is what he most wants in the world, after your authentic happiness. This is what he has told me every single painful day since he left Geneva. I tell you, my brother has been more than miserable. It's been so hard to watch."

And for me, as profoundly angry and disappointed as I've been at Ben since I discovered he left, in truth, my wish to see him and be with him again manifested at the end of every angry thought and rationalization. Every pause had this wish within it. Even when I was most hurt and rageful, my heart remembered and yearned for his kiss.

I feel like I'm dreaming, or more accurately, that I have been stuck in a nightmare and am finally, finally awakening.

Chapter Forty-Eight

As the truth and recent turn of events slowly but powerfully sink in, I subsequently start to feel free and light again, but I am also struck that I was such an incredible fool. First, I believed in Fredrick's worthiness, and then his trustworthiness, and worst of all, I believed that Ben would leave me in the dust with nothing for someone else. How did I ever believe that?

All of a sudden I think of Jacqui. Sweet Jacqui who has been so worried about me through all of this. I haven't told her. She doesn't know. I hurry to find Jacqui and Evan.

***

As I relay the story, Evan looks so disgusted by what has happened and blurts out, "No one is meaner and more spiteful than Fredrick Grange. What a jealous asshole. You could tell just from looking at him. We should never have let you go to Geneva for that man!"

But my own anger and shock have already started to evaporate and dissipate into the most hopeful of feelings. This has all been a mistake. And it can actually be rectified. This is what I had hoped in my darkest moments, that I would discover there was a reason, that he did truly love me.

I tell Evan, "Well, since it's not the Victorian age any more, you all don't actually control my life. And, the good news, is that I actually think my chances for love are looking pretty good."

While Evan still looks peeved, beside him Jacqui looks more delighted than I would have even expected and utters gleefully, "This is the most romantic tale ever! Here is mean, dull Fredrick and he sees that Ben is the one for you and that you are the one for Ben. For once, Fredrick actually instinctively knew something. I didn't give him enough credit. And then the poor sob, out of spite, tries his best to stop it with his evil plan—well, no surprise there. But is thwarted! It all gets sorted out, and true love prevails. It's awesome. It's like a movie."

I do not look as amused as Jacqui does. While I'm beyond thrilled that things are looking up, I cannot immediately forget that this ordeal has hurt me to the quick.

"Oh come on Ginny, you have to admit it's a pretty fantastic story."

"I guess I hadn't thought of it like that. I haven't had the time or distance."

"It's the story you can tell your grandkids! They'll eat it up. It's so romantic."

There's Jacqui getting ahead of herself.

"Glad you approve Jacqui. And now, I need to go find Ben."

Chapter Forty-Nine

Leila had ended our conversation by scribbling Ben's new address on a napkin for me, "just in case."

I hold the napkin in my hand like it is the holy grail. I feel nervous, anxious, hopeful and excited all at the same time. I know in my heart he wants to see me. Leila assured me of this. And I know, even with all that has transpired, and for all my trepidation, I desire more than anything to see him. Each step I take towards the apartment building feels momentous. I try to just breathe. It will unfold. I just need to get there. I just need to be present in the moment, breathe deeply, feel the sensations within me, and look into his eyes. Ben taught me all these tools. Now I will use them when I need them most.

I knock, shakily. My hand feels surreal against the door. I feel myself holding my breath. I consciously release. Ben opens the door. He looks as nervous as I feel. But when he lays his eyes on me, it all falls away. He looks deeply in my eyes and wraps his whole being around me. We stand in the doorway embraced in the strongest, most heartfelt hug I've ever experienced. What I feel most actively is the beating of my own heart as it resonates through my body and off of Ben's, feeling his in turn, echo through mine. We are an echo chamber of heartbeats.

***

"Thank goodness you are here. It's been ludicrous Ginny. Crazy. Life has been so fucking painful without you. I thought the heaven I experienced with you in Geneva had vanished forever and I just couldn't bear it."

I let the tears fall freely down my cheeks. His arms are around me. He is kissing my neck, my face, my hair. He's holding me so tightly it almost hurts, and that's how I want it. Seeing him feels like finding again that which was most precious, lost and untimely ripped from me, and then most mourned. I hold on with everything I have and everything I don't.

His deep voice resonates, "Do you have any idea how hard it is when that which you desire most in the world, that you most long for, is kept at bay by intolerable conditions?"

"I think I do," I say with a rejoiceful smile, mixed with the sweet relief that perhaps this misery and misunderstanding is in our past. "I know I do."

He smiles back. And there they are, the lines around his eyes that I have missed so profoundly. I touch and kiss them like I did in Geneva.

Ben draws me close, I feel dizzied by his ambrosial smell. His face comes close to mine, oh how I've missed that approach. He presses my head against his chest with a force I have not felt from him before. It sends gorgeous tremors throughout my body; I open my eyes to see his fiery-blues fully ablaze. I let myself hold the gaze I have missed so sincerely.

His warm, soft lips finally touch mine and my whole body clings to his kiss. I feel like I am holding on for dear life. I've lost him once, our bodies and mouths cling like magnets as if to say we will never be parted again. Time fades while the kiss unfolds; our lips are making up for lost time.

There are flowers hidden all over a woman's body, Ben once said to me. "And it's my job to discover yours, one by one." His words were poetry to me then, and I watch as he inhales the undulations of my body. We conspire, and all I can say is 'yes' over and over again. I whisper it. I breath it in; I exhale it.

He pursues me like the sun. I feel him slip my dress over my head. I'd forgotten that I was still dressed, and he is fully naked. I have almost unknowingly undressed him, so incredibly eager to see and feel his precise body again.

I bend to his nipple. So soft and sweet. It hardens in my mouth, slight and perfect amidst his beautiful chest. Circles with my tongue. I've missed his nipples. And after our re-acquaintance, with both a fervor and, for reasons I do not know, some intimidation, I bend down further and find the place between his thighs. Here is his most private body part, ready for me to hold again. I gently place my lips and kiss the tip of his cock. He stirs visibly, shakes with the pleasure. I kiss and lick and hold slowly, stalling in the most delightful way, giving us back the time. Then I fully take him in my mouth, sucking him tenderly but oh so eagerly, wanting his gorgeous cock to fill every orifice I have, because each one has missed him so much. His pleasure noises spill forth.

When he can take no more pleasure without coming, Ben lifts me up to his lips and we kiss for so long I lose my breath. When I retrieve it once again, I wrap my arms around him and pull him towards me, my breasts pressing into his chest. I can feel his heart racing too. Love and life race back into all of the scarred and broken places between us, healing each spot one lick at a time.

We are entwined, our hands, our mouths. I can feel the length of his body and the length and heat of his erection against me. He traces his tongue along my cheek, my ear... He runs his fingers through my hair. No need to rush. We have waited a very long time. He gazes down at me.

"Ginny," he whispers sweetly and gently bites my lower lip. "I missed you so much."

His tears flow with his words, and I lick them away one by one. I have never seen Ben cry before. I am so touched; it is beyond words. My tongue meets his once again and we climb into one another. He lifts me up and carries me onto the bed. He lays me down so softly and ritualistically, it's as if it's our first time.

The pulse, the heat, he licks my nipples as I tug at his hair. His mouth and hands to my breasts with true appreciation, oh those blonde curls, my fingers run through them like a bear through a honeycomb, after so much effort and longing, they are all for me.

When Ben is momentarily done nestling and nuzzling his head into my breasts, he lifts and presses my knees up, and I hook my arms around them, giving myself a hug to remind myself I am not dreaming this time. He runs his thumb down along the inside of my thigh then to my clitoris to trace glorious circles. I can feel myself getting wetter and wetter. Sitting between my legs, I look at his face. I know he loves how wet I get, for he told me so many times. With him, my body has never betrayed me. The opposite. Time and again, my wetness lets Ben know, I am wanting. And then his tongue, oh that tongue, massaging and licking and humming sweet pleasure up and down my spine. Boy, did I miss his tongue!

"Sweet Ginny," he says and licks his lips once more. "Nectar," his eyes tugging at me. "You taste so delicious."

I wrap my knees over his shoulders as he kisses and licks me like he cannot get enough. And just when I think I might combust, he enters me. Oh my stars. My eyes are closed and fill with an iridescence of light, aurora borealis. Kama moving inside of me. It is my whole universe in this one moment.

At this point, Ben seems to know my body better than I do. He has studied the energetics of my pleasure. He knows where all of my sweet flowers hide. He blooms each one as he moves through my body. Wordlessly, ineffably, we move together. His strong arms, there they are, I grab on, oh, his beautiful back, the sensation is blinding for me. I move my legs to wrap them around his waist and pull him tighter, deeper into me. I want there to be no distance at all. Only connection. It's been lonely in my body. For months, I felt unloved in all the places that Ben had awakened. But now, they enliven again, in full bloom, as if coming out of hibernation into the bright day.

"Ginny, I love you," he exhales. "I love you so much."

He looks at me igniting a burning passion in me. Our eyes lock as he thrusts into me and my movements around him gain speed, hurling us through the universe in unison, and just then, as I hear and see and feel him come, I touch the firmament behind the stars, one wonderful, Big Bang.

***

As we lie in each other's arms, in bed, delighting in the hours of just reconnecting physically, emotionally, spiritually, we also know it's time, at last, to talk. Leila had done the heavy lifting, but Ben needs to explain to me, personally, face to face body to body. He knows it too. He holds my hand as he does, just as I would want him to do.

"Ginny, I'm so sorry. I now know it was crazy, misguided in every way. On the one hand, the opportunity to make something of myself professionally, something or someone you could be proud of was one thing—that felt real. I want your respect, Ginny, I need it—it wouldn't work for us without that piece—I know that to be true; that was tantalizing in and of itself. But honestly, Ginny, when Fredrick threatened to publish your work as his, I have never felt so torn in my life. I told myself that I had to leave, which was the last thing I wanted to do, so that you could continue your path in your work, work that has meant the world to you for years—I couldn't stand in the way of your career, or worse, be responsible for its fall. I felt equally strongly that I had to go so that Fredrick wouldn't publish your work as his and that I had to stay and just love you, work be damned. I just didn't know which was ultimately more important."

As he speaks these words, the irony is not lost on us.

I look in his eyes and say, "Between love and work, Ben, make no mistake, I know, now, which one comes first."

He holds me and kisses me. I kiss him back. The softness of our lips, the electricity running through my body, reminds me of our very first kiss. For the first time since I can remember, I feel no sadness whatsoever, only the lightness and profound contentment that accompanies the sense of loving and being loved in return.

***

Following another long silent embrace in which we fully appreciate being close again, Ben pulls himself slightly away, holding my arms in his, but at a distance.

"But Ginny, really, what if Fredrick publishes the paper?"

"Ben, there's no worry there. You know me, I throw myself into my work. That's what I do. You, us, those weeks in Geneva, were a wonderful anomaly. In my deep sadness, once I could lift up my head, if I wasn't walking, or volunteering, I was writing. I read through all your notes on the copy of my dissertation. It was one of the few things you left in the apartment, one of the few things that still connected us. Your comments were astute, so helpful. I sat in the library and coffee shops and I wrote. It's done. I sent it off to readers. It made me feel better to accomplish something, something I actually had control over. Ironically, in that realm, your leaving was a godsend of sorts."

I smile, thinking that if Fredrick wants to play this game, partake in this chess match, well, he doesn't know his opponent, this queen, as well as he thinks. I am more powerful than people sometimes give me credit for; I remember my mother telling me what my kindergarten teacher told her long ago, "She may be little, but never underestimate her."

With my dissertation in so many people's hands, if Fredrick tries something stupid like his initial plan, I'll have covered my timeline bases. Others will support that my work came first. That's my cognitive and pragmatic response. The work will work itself out; it always does. I'm good at what I do. But I also respond to Ben, even more truly, with my soul,

"Ben, honestly, the more I care about us, which is more than anything, the less I care about that stuff."

He smiles the biggest smile I've yet seen grace his most beautiful face. His smile lines appear. I lean in for a kiss and I know we will be okay. Better than okay. We have incredible love and work, in that order. We will be fantastic.

CPSIA information can be obtained
at www.ICGtesting.com
Printed in the USA
FSHW02n1943030718
50129FS